THE BLACKSMITH'S MAIL ORDER BRIDE

CINDY CALDWELL

PRICKLY PEAR PRESS

Copyright © 2016 by Cindy Caldwell

All rights reserved.

No part of this book may be reproduced in any form or by any electronic or mechanical means, including information storage and retrieval systems, without written permission from the author, except for the use of brief quotations in a book review.

If you'd like to receive my new release alerts, special promos, giveaways and early release discounts, sign up for my mailing list at:

Cindy Caldwell New Release Alerts

CHAPTER 1

Olivia swept the last of the dust off the side of the porch and peeked up under the awning. Just in time. The wind would be picking up any minute now and she shielded her eyes against the blazing sun. Thunderheads rolled over the tops of the mountains to the east over Tombstone and they'd be here in no time.

Across the pasture, Percy shooed the cows they had left into the pen and tipped his hat back as he secured the latch for the night. He turned at the first roll of thunder and squinted toward the mountains, pulling his hat back down, his head lowered as he walked quickly back toward the barn.

Percy. He never talked much, not even when her pa was alive. She'd tried to talk him out of hiring the scrawny older man with the perpetual twitch in his eye, but her pa's words rang in her ears once more.

"You're going to need help when I pass, Liv. I know he isn't the finest specimen of a man, but he's been a friend of mine since I was a boy and we need the help. I'm not going to be around forever."

She'd relented as her father's condition deteriorated far more rapidly than she'd hoped. Her mother's death had been long and grueling—what she could remember of it as she'd been much younger when it happened—but it wasn't something easily forgotten, even if it had been long ago.

She and her father had managed on the ranch alone quite nicely for many years, and it had been a truly joyful time. The passing of the seasons—what there was of them out here in the high desert of Arizona—always pleased her, and now that the monsoons were coming—well, it was the time of year that she felt her father with her most. It was his favorite time of year. The pork was curing by then and there wasn't too much work to be done until it was time to take it all to market, so the many hours they'd spent on the porch watching the lightning and listening to the patter of raindrops were times she'd been happiest. They'd taken turns reading to each other until it was too dark to stay out, and after a simple meal—she was a pretty good cook, if she did say so herself—they'd sit by the fire until it was time to retire.

Her shoulders sagged as she leaned her chin on the handle of the broom, turning toward Percy as he reached the steps of the porch.

"Looks like it's going to storm," he said slowly, his eye twitching as it always did.

She brushed her forehead with the back of her hand and wound her long, brown hair tighter into its bun. She wished she could still wear braids—heck, it didn't even matter out here where she rarely saw a person other than Percy, she didn't think—but she shoved the pins in more tightly as she decided that yes, tomorrow it would be a braid. Ever practical, a trait she'd inherited from her father, buns were for the birds and she decided right then and there that even though she'd be thought a schoolgirl, she didn't care.

"Yes, it certainly does," she replied as a bolt of lightning crossed the sky. She jumped at its accompanying crack of thunder and Percy turned back toward her.

"Did you close up the smokehouse, Percy? We all set to ride this out?"

Percy reached in his trousers and pulled out a

handkerchief, rubbing it slowly over his face as the raindrops started to fall. "Yes, ma'am. All buttoned up for now and the fuel all prepared for the next few days. Shouldn't need to go back to Tombstone for quite a while."

"Thank you for going in today. It's getting so I don't even want to leave the ranch much anymore, so I appreciate you heading in for supplies."

"No problem, ma'am, and I'm glad you didn't go. Saw some Indians on the way back. Must not have been Apache or I'd be dead. They kept a wide berth but it gave me a bit of a scare."

Olivia looked out over the horizon, her heart beating a little faster. They'd had several visits from Indians over the years but not recently, and she didn't want that to change. She supposed it was good that they'd had a bumper crop of hogs and were expert at curing the meat they provided. It did invite interest from Indians and white men alike, but they'd had enough run-ins that for the last several years, people had steered clear.

"You don't think they'll be trying to..."

Percy shook his head quickly. "No. The reputation of the Double Barrel Ranch is a good one, and nobody seems willing to talk about stealing a thing. I

THE BLACKSMITH'S MAIL ORDER BRIDE

was just mentioning it so you could be on the lookout, just in case."

"Thank you, Percy." She glanced at the shotgun leaning against the front door and realized she hadn't had to use it for quite some time. She supposed the times she'd had to in the past—and hadn't hesitated one bit to protect the ranch—had people still talking. She banked on that, that no one was willing to rob them—or to try to, anyway, because of the consequence of getting a rear end full of buckshot.

She turned her attention from her memories back to Percy as he spoke again. "But I think it might be good for you to go in once in a while. A lovely young lady like you needs company—of her own age and possibly of the male persuasion."

Percy didn't customarily speak much and her eyebrows rose at this—what would equal a week's worth of words, normally.

Color rose in his cheeks as he kicked the dirt. She'd been grateful Percy was around and he had been a good friend to her father. They'd even taken weekly trips into Tombstone, sometimes spending the night, during that last year of his life. She was grateful that her father had had the opportunity to get out and about. But he'd never to date given his opinion about much of anything. Well, not anything, really, that didn't involve the smokehouse.

"I appreciate the sentiment, Percy, but I don't have time for things like that. Nor the interest." She glanced over toward Tombstone, thinking of how quickly it had grown. She'd even heard that there was a bowling alley next to the theater that ran all year long, all day and all night for the miners who were on different shifts. She might like to see it one day, but she shook the thought from her head.

"Supper shouldn't be more than an hour. I'll ring for you when it's time," she said as she turned to go into the clapboard house her father had built with his bare hands.

"Anything I can help with?" He looked up at the sky and stomped his boots, which would soon be covered in mud.

"No, thank you. Rabbit stew tonight and biscuits are already made. I'll see you in a little bit."

As Percy headed toward his quarters in the barn, her eyes drifted to the small hill on the far side of the pasture, the bright yellow of the flowers she kept on the tidy graves catching her eye. She thought maybe tomorrow she'd take some new ones, for both graves, and she plopped onto the wooden rocker as she rubbed her forehead.

The clouds moved quickly toward her, and she imagined the streets of Tombstone must be rivers by now, the flash floods coming down from the hills that surrounded it. She could see it, Tombstone—although it was a decent ride away, quite a few miles. She didn't get in often and wondered if maybe she should try to get in more—especially now that the meat was put up and curing for a while and things on the ranch were calm.

Actually, she said a brief prayer of gratitude that things *were* calm out here for her. She was, in fact, a woman trying to keep a ranch and a business going on her own. She had Percy, certainly, to help but it could get a little lonely these days. Percy wasn't near the conversationalist her father had been and a month or two after her father died, she'd quit trying.

A squall settled over Tombstone in the distance, and she laughed as she imagined the ladies in their finery, the feathers in their hats flying as they ran for cover through puddles and puddles of mud. Maybe they had a man who would take off his cape and throw it over a puddle for her so as not to sully her boots.

She shook her head as Percy closed the door to the barn behind him, stopping to blow his nose loudly in his handkerchief. He didn't even own a rain cape, she imagined.

Her father did and would have been one to help a lady on the rare occasions it was necessary. "Just because we live out on a ranch doesn't mean you're not a lady, Olivia. Don't ever forget that."

She laughed out loud as she gazed down at her dirty hands and stained apron from her day's work. A lady? Hardly. Nor did she want to be.

Glancing back at Tombstone, she was glad that she wasn't standing on the boardwalk waiting for someone to throw down a cape so she could cross. No. She was practical. She'd take care of it on her own, feathered hat or not. She would just walk to the other side of the street and deal with the consequences afterward.

Just like now. She'd go inside, light the fire, clean up and provide a perfectly decent meal. Just like she'd done for years.

CHAPTER 2

*J*oe Stanton leaned his head against the closed door of the blacksmith shop that he owned with his brother, Will, and pinched the bridge of his nose. He turned the sign around, "Closed" now showing toward Allen Street, one of the busiest streets in Tombstone.

He wiped soot from his hands and threw the soiled rag into the washbasin. He realized he'd barely spoken to a soul all day and while that sometimes was a very good thing, he missed having his brother, Will, there with him in the shop their father had left them when he'd died.

He supposed he should be grateful for the silence —especially when he still had to go home to their ma, who could talk the bark off a tree. Wouldn't be so bad if it was something interesting but it usually wasn't. Lately, it had mostly been how upset she was about Carol and Will getting married. As Joe didn't share her opinions even a little bit—he loved Carol, and had never seen Will happier—he mostly tried to avoid her when he could.

Tonight, though, there'd be no avoiding her. He'd agreed to meet his aunt and mother at the Occidental for supper. The only reason he *had* was because Will had been the only decent cook in the house and since he'd left, Joe felt like he'd been starving to death. A decent meal at the Occidental, the best restaurant in town owned by old friends, was worth putting up with just about anything.

That's what he'd thought, anyway, when he'd said he'd meet his mother and aunt there at six o'clock. As he locked the door to the shop and stepped outside, he looked both ways up the boardwalk as water rushed by and the rain pounded the dirt. He inhaled deeply, the smell of rain one of his favorites since childhood. He didn't even mind that the streets of Tombstone looked like rivers as the heavy rain commenced and thunder cracked over the town. Monsoon season, one of his favorite times of the year, was in full swing and he never minded how wet he got.

The storms would come and go quickly for the next few months in the high desert and he looked forward to how green things would become, almost the opposite of other places he'd visited where in summer, all the plants turned brown. Not here.

He turned up his collar and headed toward the Occidental, his stomach grumbling already. As he'd done his repetitive work today and hammered horseshoes, rotating them back and forth from the fiery forge and the water barrel, he'd already been trying to decide what he'd order. Tripp and Sadie's restaurant was famous for unusual dishes and he wondered what might be on special tonight. If it wasn't something he just had to try, he'd already settled on Tripp's trail stew and biscuits, a favorite of all the ranch hands that had ridden the trail with him and one of Joe's favorites as well.

Joe slowed as he approached the Occidental. He'd grabbed his cloak at the last minute, hoping to stay a little dry as he'd be going to the restaurant, and he saw his mother and aunt had done the same thing. They stood on the boardwalk outside the restaurant next to a covered buggy, and Joe stopped dead in his tracks.

His stomach dropped and he closed his eyes tight, hoping that in the buggy would be someone—

anyone—but his cousins. As much as his mother babbled, you'd think she would have mentioned that *they* would be there. Or maybe she'd finally understood what he'd decided long ago—that where they were, he wouldn't be. If he'd known they were coming, he'd have gone home and had a hard biscuit or even a lump of coal for supper. Anything was better than his cousins.

"Joseph, how lovely to see you," his aunt Dorothy —or the Widow Samson, as most people in Tombstone called her—said as she held out her limp hand to him and leaned on her cane with the other.

Joe glared at his mother who looked quickly away, her smile wide as she bent over to peer into the carriage.

"Look who's here, Joseph. Trudy and Taffy and Tracy, all three." His mother held up her hand and wiggled her fingers toward the carriage. Joe cringed as his cousins stood.

Trudy, the oldest, sounding just like her mother, said, "How lovely to see you, Joseph. I haven't seen you since—well, since—"

Joe was glad she'd just stopped, as he knew full well what she meant. None of them had seen each other since Will and Carol's wedding, and what a disaster that had been. For him, anyway, and his heart ached at the way his family had treated his brother's new bride. He was grateful that she and Will were so in love that they only had eyes for each other, and hadn't noticed the disrespect and downright rudeness of his family.

He wasn't at all surprised when she lifted her nose in the air and her eyebrows rose as she looked down at Joseph on the boardwalk. He thanked his lucky stars that he'd grabbed his cape at the first crack of thunder before he'd locked the door of the shop. He knew exactly what she wanted, and knew she'd stand there in the carriage until she got it.

"Joseph," his mother prodded as his aunt stood by, her eyebrows raised as well as she tapped her cane on the planks of the boardwalk...a sound he'd hated since he was a child.

He sighed and looked up at his cousins as they all stood watching him, their parasols ready for when they needed them. He unbuttoned his cape and laid it down on the mud between the carriage and the steps of the boardwalk, extending a hand to each of them in turn.

His three cousins were safely on the boardwalk as he reached down to retrieved his muddy cape and he stopped when he heard his aunt clear her throat. He looked up at her and she nodded to the carriage.

Confused, he turned toward the buggy and looked up into the eyes of a young woman he'd never met before.

"Beautiful, isn't she?" his cousin Taffy whispered in his ear. He reached up, taking her gloved hand in his as he helped her down. It felt cold even through the leather, and as she smiled vacantly and batted her eyelashes at him, he couldn't quite look her in the eye. If she was anything like his cousins, beauty wouldn't save her.

With the gaggle of ladies safely on the boardwalk, he collected his cape and walked behind the buggy to shake it out. Clumps of mud flew as it dripped in the street, and he rested it over the bench outside the restaurant, hoping it would dry by the time they'd finished supper. The rain had just stopped and a ray of sun poked through the clouds—although it did nothing to lighten his mood.

When he returned to the group, his cousin Tracy reached for his elbow and steered him straight toward the woman he'd helped down from the buggy last.

"Joseph, I'd like you to meet my friend, Jasmine Bartholomew, who's recently arrived from New Orleans. We met when I was traveling. She's come to visit and to—look around," she said, snickering behind her hand as she winked at Jasmine.

Joe tugged at his collar as he tipped his hat at the young lady. "How do you do, ma'am? It's a pleasure to meet you," he said, although he most certainly did not think it was a pleasure at all. He looked around at his cousins, each smiling smugly—expressions that matched his aunt's and his mother's.

Like a bull heading to slaughter, he held the door open for the ladies—were they ladies, really? Carol was a true lady, in his estimation. These women were...well, they'd tricked him, for one, and it wasn't fair. Especially without his brother. He was unprotected, easy prey.

"Joseph, you sit next to Jasmine, right here," Taffy said as she maneuvered him next to their friend. "She can tell you all about New Orleans and about herself. She's fascinating, really."

Joseph plopped into his seat and rubbed the back of his neck. For the next hour, Jasmine tittered and regaled him with unwelcome information about her life in the most horrid, screechy voice he'd ever heard. If this was any indication of how things were going to go, he would have been much better off with the stale bread and water for supper—and wished he had chosen just that.

CHAPTER 3

Olivia wiped her forehead with the sleeve of her worn, calico dress, swiping at the salty beads that streamed down her face. It was so dusty here she never seemed to have a clean face, or clean hands. But it was the ranch she'd been born on and she had no intention of leaving, not even now.

The cold, hard steel of the gun in her hand was comforting. In the hands of most people, it wouldn't seem like much against the three riders she'd seen before she grabbed for it, making sure it was loaded as she crouched beneath the kitchen window. But she'd learned from the best, and knew she could hold her own better than most.

She threw a handful of extra shells in the pocket of her dingy, gray apron and waited. The dirt floor shook with the thud of hooves as the trio of riders approached. She squeezed her eyes shut once more, wishing her pa were here to help her—at least take another shotgun and another vantage point. Then they might have a chance, and they'd done it plenty of times before. When her pda was alive, riders like this had steered clear of the Double Barrel ranch, hearing tell of the fate their compadres had met when they'd tried messing with the Blanchards. She only hoped that this time would be fast, and they'd either be on their way or not able to be. She was fine with either ending.

She stood slowly, avoiding the window, and headed to the front door.

"Olivia? Please don't make trouble. Just give them what they want." The older man dropped the curtain and stepped back from the window and shoved a lock of gray hair from his wrinkled face.

"Shush, Percy. I know what I'm doing," she said as she peeked out the window one last time and the horses galloped through the gates of the ranch. They'd soon reach the house, and she knew she needed to be ready.

Cradling the shotgun in the crook of her arm, she took one last peek at Percy and glared at him.

The riders didn't slow their horses until the last

minute She stifled a cough at the cloud of dust and tried to stand as stock still as she could. "Hold your own, Liv," her pa had told her hundreds of times. "And you do that with more than just a gun. Your face, your shoulders, your voice. But you gotta do it if you're gonna live out here."

She squinted up at the man in front as the three glared down at her, handkerchiefs covering the bottom of their faces. She sighed as she recognized the worn leather saddle of Jimmy Joe Walker, and again, if the situation hadn't been so dicey she'd have laughed. What good does it do to wear a handkerchief over your face to be incognito yet ride for some dirty deed with your saddle branded with your initials, JJW? Not that it mattered. Everybody in these parts knew Jimmy Joe Walker for the coward he was.

"Hate to ride up on you like this, Miss Blanchard, but we hear you have something we want, and we plan to take it."

"Is that right, Mr. Walker?" Olivia asked as she hitched the gun up further on her hip and his eyes grew bigger over the blue handkerchief that was tied to cover his nose and mouth.

He slapped his thigh and pulled the handkerchief from his mouth as the other men did the same.

"Dadgummit, Olivia, how'd you know it was me?" he said as he leaned forward on the horn of the saddle—just above his initials branded into the leather.

Percy stepped closer behind her, his own shotgun resting loose in his hand. Olivia didn't mind now that she knew who the men were—in fact, Percy and her father had played poker sometimes with Walker, so maybe Percy could talk some sense into him.

"It wasn't difficult," she said as she thrust her chin toward his saddle. He sat up quickly and let out a sigh as he spied his own initials.

"Oh, right. That," he said as he wiped his forehead with his handkerchief. "Next time I'll borrow a saddle from somebody else."

"Next time?" she said as she gripped the shotgun more tightly. "What do you want, anyway? You're not getting Pa's inventory. I've told you that before. It's promised to the mercantile in Tombstone."

"Now, now, Olivia, I believe I can offer you a sight more than Suzanne and James. Don't you want to make as much money as you can?"

Olivia looked past Walker's straggly brown hair and dirt streaked face to the two mounds marked with crosses on the far side of the smokehouse. Olivia and her father had negotiated a price with the mercantile before he'd passed last spring, and it was a fair one. They'd been selling their smoked ham and bacon there for years, and as this was the last batch she and her pa had set up together, she had every intention of honoring his wishes.

She reached in her pocket and felt for the note that her father had left her that said just that and she turned back to Jimmy Joe Walker.

"Pa was very clear about what he wanted me to do, Mr. Walker, and I'm going to do it."

Walker scowled at her as he tugged his hat and slapped it on his thigh. He let out a sigh and picked up the reins he'd wrapped around the horn of his saddle as his horse shuffled in the dirt.

"Percy, can't you talk some sense into this woman?" he said as he studied the dirt under his fingernails.

Olivia's eyebrows rose as she turned to Percy. He shrugged at her and turned his wide eyes to Walker.

"I don't see how I could, Jimmy. Mr. Blanchard was pretty clear."

Walker rubbed the back of his neck and looked over at the smokehouse. "That inventory would be worth a whole lot more in Tucson. You two know that. And I'd be happy to be the middle man."

Olivia let out a sigh. She'd told him no at least

three times, and it didn't seem he was ever going to understand. She lifted the shotgun up higher and aimed it in his direction.

"I'm going to say this one more time. No."

He sat up tall in the saddle, his palms held out toward her. "All right, all right. I see you don't want to discuss it any further today. We'll let you get back to your day, ma'am," he said as he tipped his hat in her direction, his gold front tooth shining with his attempt at a smile.

He nodded his head toward his men and turned his horse back toward the gate. "Let me know when you change your mind," he said over his shoulder as he spurred the horse down the canyon that led to the ranch.

CHAPTER 4

Olivia reached for her gloves and shoved them into her pocket. She'd been dreading this trip for days—for the most part. She didn't like to go into town much at all, but was glad that she at least would get to see her friends, Sadie and Suzanne, as it was time to discuss the meat that would be ready soon.

The thought crossed her mind that maybe she should take Percy with her—hadn't he mentioned he'd seen Indians a while back on his last trip to town? Yes, she thought he had. But instead of inviting Percy to come with her, she reached for the double-barreled shotgun instead. She'd be just fine, and Percy needed to stay and watch over things at the ranch. With all that meat in the smokehouse—

worth a pretty penny, at that—she couldn't afford to leave the ranch unattended.

The ride into town took a fair while, and she took care to leave as soon as the sun came up so she'd be able to make it home the same day. Sometimes, she spent the night at a hotel but today, she hadn't wanted to take the time—or spend the money. She jingled the meager coins in her reticule—not many to spare this time of year.

The crystal blue sky held for her entire trip and she hoped that today wouldn't be a heavy monsoon day, even though she'd chosen to bring the covered buggy just in case. She'd actually enjoyed the trip, traveling down from the mountains into the valley, crossing the San Pedro River and ascending the small hills that surrounded Tombstone.

By the time she arrived at the mercantile, she was quite hungry. And even though she was counting her pennies for a few more weeks, the alluring aroma wafting from the Occidental convinced her she'd at least need a meat pie for her trip back, Sadie's specialty.

A plume of dust crept up her nose as the horses shook off the wear of the ride. Olivia sneezed and pulled her handkerchief from the long sleeve of her dress. Wiping the dust from her face, she squared her shoulders, warding off the shiver that washed over her as she remembered the visit from that ridiculous Mr. Walker. Just a few more days, she reminded herself, and it would all be over. For this year, at least. If she could make arrangements with Sadie and Suzanne and Percy could hold down the fort, she'd have some breathing room for the rest of the year and the ranch would be safe.

The white handkerchief was covered in dust by the time she'd poured some water into it and wiped her face as clean as she could. Maybe a bit of rain would have been helpful, although then she'd be sopping wet. It was always one or the other, it seemed, living on the ranch. Covered in dust or soaking wet.

She gathered her reticule and the list of available inventory she'd carefully written out by candlelight the night before and prepared herself for her negotiations with Suzanne. It really wasn't much of a negotiation, really, since her father had built the business and it was more of an annual ritual. But she wanted to be ready as this was the first year she'd done it on her own. She'd accompanied her father and knew what to ask about, but this was her first time meeting with the owners of the mercantile alone. Yes, they were friends, but business was business.

She looked up and down the street, wondering about leaving her shotgun in the back of the buggy while she stepped inside. Her stomach grumbled again as she caught a whiff of Sadie's meat pies wafting from the door of the Occidental restaurant next door. As she shuffled the papers and her bag in her arms and turned to head on inside, she hung her head at the familiar voice from the man standing on the boardwalk.

"Well, pretty lady. Guess you're here to talk about the inventory at Double Barrel Ranch," Jimmy Joe Walker said as he hooked his thumbs in his worn, leather belt. "I'm open for any discussion you might wish to have. About anything."

Her stomach turned as he winked at her, his greasy hair falling over his eyes. Olivia slowly untied her bonnet and removed it carefully, setting it on the seat of the buggy. She flipped her braids over her shoulder—she hadn't bothered to pin her hair up today—and was glad she hadn't. She'd learned long ago that the wide brim didn't help much with visibility, and from the sound of the man's voice, she'd need to see what was coming at her. She never expected this kind of thing when she was in town, and her stomach clenched as she reached over into the back of the buggy and rested her hand on her shotgun.

Her fingers played over the cool steel as she looked up into the eyes of the man who'd addressed her and smiled.

"Good day, Mr. Walker. How unusual to see you here in town rather than at the ranch for a change."

Walker took a step back and squinted at Olivia. She quickly looked up and down the boardwalk, and realized that he'd likely not been expecting her as his ruffians weren't with him.

"Why, Olivia, I just came out to have a friendly conversation. Your father and I were friends, after all. And of course, Percy and I go way back."

She stifled a laugh and took another glance down the boardwalk. He couldn't possibly be so stupid that he didn't realize her father would never befriend the likes of him. He was horrid from head to toe, including the belly that drooped down over his belt buckle with his initials on it.

"Don't believe you've been invited since Pa died, and I'd thank you to remember that before you come out again. You're not welcome. Not to talk about the inventory or anything else." She gripped the barrel of the shotgun and wiggled the fingers of her free hand, hoping he wouldn't force the issue here. Right in the middle of Allen Street, the busiest one in Tombstone.

He took a step forward as he glared down at her from the boardwalk, his black eyes flashing. "Now you see here, missy. Your father promised me that..."

Olivia knew full well her father had promised no such thing, even though Percy had suggested they might try to strike a deal with Walker, one that might be better than what she could get from Suzanne. But she knew it wasn't true—she had the last letter her father had written to prove it, although she'd not shown it to anyone. She reached into her sleeve and felt the comforting crinkle of paper, just to make sure she'd brought it with her.

"Is there a problem here?"

Olivia looked up quickly to see who'd spoken, and her eyes widened at the sight of the two brothers who owned the blacksmith shop. She'd stopped in a few times, but neither one of them had spoken much. She'd heard that Will, the younger brother, had recently married a girl in a chair with wheels but she hadn't been into town for a long time. Percy'd told her after he'd returned several weeks ago.

Next to him stood his brother—what was his

name? Joe? She couldn't remember, but she didn't need either one of them interfering in her business.

"Thank you, no. Mr. Walker will be moving along now." Olivia lifted the shotgun out of the buggy as she sighed. It seemed no matter what she tried, there had been trouble since her father passed. He'd hoped Percy could help her, but he'd turned out to be as lazy as the other hands they'd hired. Seemed she just needed to do things on her own.

"I beg to differ, Miss Blanchard. We do, indeed, have business to discuss," Walker said as he turned to glare at the blacksmiths.

She hitched the shotgun on her hip, pointing it at the ground for now, but prepared to do whatever she needed to do to get this man out of her way. She'd come to meet with Suzanne and conclude her business, and she wouldn't let anyone—especially a scoundrel like this—stand in her way.

Walker took a step forward and leaned in. "Don't think just because we're in town I can't make my wishes known, young lady."

"Hold on there, Mr. Walker," the younger blacksmith said as he walked forward, his palms outward.

"Take a step back," his brother said as he followed behind. He glanced at Olivia as he cocked his head and pushed his hat up on his forehead.

Walker blinked a couple of times as he stared at Olivia, and then he looked up at the two brothers. He broke into a smile and Olivia thought maybe it was the most insincere one she'd ever seen as he held his hands out toward the men, palms out.

"Nothing going on here, gentlemen. Just having a little friendly conversation with the lady. I'll be on my way." He nodded at Olivia as he turned away from the mercantile. "We can continue our conversation at a later date, Miss Blanchard."

Olivia thrust out her chin and squared her shoulders. "Nothing to talk about. Don't bother," she said as he headed down Allen Street, frowning as he glanced at the blacksmiths over his shoulder.

"You all right, ma'am?" the younger brother asked as he strode down the wooden stairs of the boardwalk, his boots raising another plume of dust.

Olivia nodded and smiled up at him. "Yes, thank you. I'd have been fine, but it seems that he scooted along faster since you arrived."

"I imagine the shotgun didn't hurt," the other brother—Joe—said. Both he and his brother hadn't taken their eyes off her gun and she frowned down at it.

"I suppose it didn't hurt, no." She looked up at Joe and cocked her head. His soft, brown eyes shifted from the shotgun to hers. Why would they be so interested in her shotgun? They were blacksmiths—surely they saw and worked on guns all the time?

Either way, she supposed it had been helpful to have them help hustle Walker on his way. Her father had warned her about him, and until the inventory was safely at the mercantile, she preferred not to see him—at all.

CHAPTER 5

Joe Stanton followed his brother into the Occidental restaurant but couldn't help but take one last look at the young woman in the street as she placed her shotgun back in the buggy and covered it with a blanket. She was vaguely familiar to him but he wasn't quite sure where he'd met her before. It was likely in the blacksmith shop, and as he thought of it, he did remember that he'd been struck several times by her deep, green eyes and confident manner. Now, once again as she stared down Jimmy Joe Walker.

He tore his attention away from her with some difficulty, wondering what her altercation with that no-good Walker had been about. He was well known for shady dealings and high-handed tactics, and had been on the wrong side of the law more than once. But he'd never been run out of town as his mother and aunt had often wished for—sometimes quite adamantly at town hall meetings, he remembered. With what he knew about the man, he was pretty sure that he was up to no good with the young lady, and wished he could have helped a little more.

He would have if needed, but every time he thought to step into something that seemed like it was going south, his mother's voice rang in his ears. "Your father was always helping people, and look where it got him. Just leave well enough alone, Joe. It never turns out right."

He took off his hat and pushed the thought from his mind. He smiled at Sadie and inhaled deeply, his stomach grumbling. Will and Carol had been in Chicago for several weeks as Will trained in silversmithing, and he'd been working long, hard hours alone at the shop. When Will came in and offered an opportunity to hear about the trip and a lunch at the Occidental, he'd jumped at the chance.

"It's great to see you, Sadie," Will said as he nodded in Sadie's direction, his eyebrows rose as he looked everywhere but her swelling belly.

"Nice to see you, too, Will. Haven't seen you

since the wedding. How's Carol, and how was your time in Chicago?"

Will cleared his throat as he looked at Joe. "It was quite an experience. Carol was able to see a couple of doctors and, of course, with the new chair we were able to see the sights. Chicago is quite an interesting town. Growing quite quickly."

Sadie smiled and rubbed her hand slowly over her apron. "I haven't been gone all that long, but I bet I wouldn't even recognize it."

She reached for menus and looked around the restaurant for an empty table. Her husband, Tripp, poked his head from the swinging door to the kitchen and frowned when his eyes found his wife.

Sadie laughed and turned back toward the brothers. "I'll put you out of your misery and let you know that yes, the baby should be coming fairly soon and no, I shouldn't be home in bed and yes, I truly enjoy hostessing at the restaurant when I can. This way, I still get to see my favorite people," she said as she waved at them to follow her to their table.

Joe exchanged a glance with Will and smiled. Having been raised by his mother and his aunt, the outspoken Widow Samson, he was accustomed to ladies with forthright opinions and statements...but wasn't at all sure about the baby information.

He wasn't quite sure how to respond and looked toward his brother. He'd been married for a while, now, and he likely knew much more about the fairer sex than he did. Shoot, he hadn't even known what to say to the damsel in distress out on the street. Although she hadn't appeared to be in that much distress, truth be told.

They took their menus from Sadie and settled into their chairs next to the window looking out to the boardwalk. Will turned and peered down Allen Street in a direction that was very familiar.

Joe laughed and clapped his brother on the back. "Carol must be back at the library, since you can't seem to keep your eyes off of it."

Will turned his startled expression back toward his brother. "Is it that obvious?"

"It has always been obvious since you laid eyes on that girl. How is she, by the way? How was your trip?"

Will's eyes softened as he looked down at the ring on his left hand. "She's fine, Will, never better. The trip was quite a success, I'd say, and we loved getting to know Chicago."

Joe leaned back in his chair and took a good look at his brother. He seemed happy and rested, even after a long trip halfway across the country. Married life must agree with him, he thought, even if it had come at a hefty price.

He hadn't wanted to bring up the subject of their mother. He still couldn't believe that she'd never accepted the fact that Will had chosen to marry Carol, one of the sweetest girls he'd ever met, just because she couldn't walk. Will had stuck to his decision, though, and Joe had never been more proud of his little brother. It was just a topic he and his mother never spoke about, and Joe was reticent to bring it up now. He should have known that he and Will were just as close as ever, and Will would know what he was thinking.

"So, how's Ma? Things are going well over at our new little house with Saffron and Adam. It's nice to have them nearby, although Carol and I enjoy our time alone. I'm glad that she can be surrounded by people who love her rather than our mother and aunt."

"And don't forget cousins," Joe said, the memory of his recent ambush still fresh in his mind.

"Cousins?" Will said as he set his menu on the side of the table. "What are they up to now?"

Joe quickly recounted the horrid evening with his brother who was in stitches by the time he was done and wiped away tears of laughter with his linen napkin.

"Oh, brother. You're in trouble now. It's begun, and it'll be like a runaway train until you settle on someone."

Joe rubbed the back of his neck. "I thought maybe your wedding would quiet things down for a while, but it seems as though it's just stoked the fire."

"It may have done if my wedding was suitable and would bring grandchildren—you know that's all she and Aunt Dorothy have been talking about for years—but the jury's still out on that one. So I guess you're on the firing line now, brother," Will said as he nudged Joe with his elbow.

The blood drained from Joe's face as he pictured not just life with that woman they'd tried to foist on him, let alone little ones with the same screechy voices all running beneath his feet.

"Oh, no. I'm not the marrying type and nobody says I have to be. Especially not to that hoity, giggly non-stop talker they introduced me to."

"Carol talks a lot. I've grown quite fond of hearing her voice, and what she has to say," Will said softly.

Sadie stepped up to the table and rested her hand on Will's shoulder. "Yes, you and Carol are the perfect match, Will. You were quite fortunate that you met."

Joe twisted his napkin at the thought of Jasmine. "Yes, they were lucky. There aren't many women here in Tombstone, what with all the single miners, and the ones I've seen, I'm either related to or they're happily married—or they're like Jasmine."

Sadie cocked her head and trained her blue eyes on Joe for a moment before she spoke. "You know, I'd never met Tripp before we agreed to marry. He needed a wife in a hurry, and Suzanne vouched for him. We couldn't be happier. If you need to get out of your mother's trap, you could consider it, as well. Suzanne and I could help," she said as she waved the waitress over.

"Oh, I—I couldn't do that," Joe said as he folded his napkin and set it on his lap.

"Why not, Joe? It would get you out of mother's sights in a hurry, that's for sure."

"I can't imagine how she'd take that after the way she reacted to *your* wedding. Marry someone I don't know? She'd likely die."

Sadie's eyes twinkled as she turned toward the kitchen. "Just let me know if you change your mind, Joe. It might help. It helped Tripp," she said as she gestured around the restaurant and pushed through the swinging door.

Joe turned toward the window and shuddered as none other than that wretched friend of his cousin's exited the Tombstone Public Library and headed in their direction.

CHAPTER 6

Olivia took one last look both ways down Allen Street and, seeing no sign of Jimmy Joe Walker, tucked the final corner of the blanket over her shotgun. She picked up the papers and her reticule once again and headed into the mercantile, stomping some of the dust off her boots before she pushed open the wide, oak door.

She fumbled around her collar for the strings of her bonnet before she remembered she'd left it in the buggy. She shrugged her shoulders and peered inside, figuring that as she was in the establishment now, there was no sense going back outside for her bonnet that she should have been wearing—outside. Seemed like a waste of time and effort to her, and there were other things to get done.

"Olivia, come in. Come in." Suzanne smiled broadly and waved Olivia inside as she walked toward her, arms spread wide. "It's been ages. We've been wondering when you'd come in to talk about this year's yield, Sadie and I. We've been looking forward to seeing you."

Heat crept into Olivia's cheeks as Suzanne wrapped her in a hug. She'd known her for a few years and remembered when she'd had her twins—Lucy and Lily must be around school age by now—but she'd never gotten used to how friendly people in town could be. But she took in a deep breath and returned Suzanne's hug as best she knew how.

She stepped back and frowned as Suzanne squinted at her and reached a hand up to push back a long, brown curl that had escaped from her braid. She rested her hands on her hips as her eyes traveled over Olivia's face.

Olivia raised her hand to her cheek. "What is it? I must look a fright after the long ride in from the ranch."

"A little more than usual, I must say," Suzanne said as she reached for a cloth on the counter.

"Oh, dear. I do apologize," Olivia said as she swiped at the dust on her face once more.

"Apologize? Whatever for? It's a long ride from the ranch with a lot of dust in between. At least you didn't get caught in a squall and it's dust, not mud," Suzanne said. She smiled and nodded at Olivia as she passed her back the dirtied cloth.

Olivia reached into her bag and pulled out the neatly folded papers she'd carefully prepared and held them out toward Suzanne. "I know this is the first time I've done this on my own, Suzanne, so I'll appreciate some of your patience."

She lowered her dark eyelashes, wishing her father were with her now and could have looked over the figures. She knew she'd done a good job of it, but it would have been nice to have someone to talk things over with. Percy certainly didn't fit the bill.

Suzanne pushed the papers back toward Olivia. "Hang on to those for a moment. Sadie's expecting us for lunch. I figured you'd want a meat pie—or anything you'd like, really. I can imagine that cooking for yourself all the time can get tiresome, so we'd like you to join us."

Olivia's stomach grumbled as if on cue and her hand flew to her stomach.

"I'll take that to mean you'll be happy to. Sadie

will need to see what you have available this season as well, for the restaurant, so we may as well wait for her to go over things." Suzanne looked around the mercantile and spotted her husband as she reached for her shawl. "James, Olivia and I are joining Sadie for lunch. I'll be back shortly."

Suzanne's tall, lanky husband poked his head out of the office and smiled at Olivia. "Hello, Olivia. Hope you've got some wonderful things for us this season." He turned to his wife and said, "Would you mind bringing me a meat pie when you return?" He smiled sheepishly at his wife, who nodded.

"Of course. I'd planned to," Suzanne said as she opened the door for Olivia and gestured for her to precede her.

"You look happy, Suzanne. Are things going well at the mercantile?" Olivia asked as she opened the door to the Occidental Restaurant next door to the mercantile.

"Things are fine with us," Suzanne said as they entered the restaurant. "The girls are in school, which I can hardly believe and Sadie—well, Sadie..."

"And Sadie is going to have a baby," Suzanne's identical twin sister said as she came around from behind the counter.

"And soon, I might add," Suzanne said as she and Olivia followed Sadie to a table.

"Goodness, Sadie, it sure does seem like it'd be soon," Olivia said as she and Suzanne followed her to a table.

"Yes, soon. But I have been feeling wonderful and I love being here. Nice chance to have lunch with you, too."

Sadie slowed as she passed by a table and stopped next to one by the window. "Suzanne, look who's back," she said, gesturing to the two men that had come to Olivia's aid earlier. There was no mistaking that they were brothers, both with wavy dark hair and deep brown eyes, tall and handsome.

They both stood as the ladies stopped and nodded toward each of them.

"Good day, ladies," the younger brother said.

"Oh, Will, how good to see you. You and Carol were in Chicago so long, it seemed. We must plan something so we can all hear about your trip." Suzanne nodded at Will's brother and smiled. "And Joe, it's always nice to see you out of the shop. How is your mother?"

It seemed to Olivia that Joe stiffened as he glanced at Will. "She's fine. Nothing different there," he said.

Will turned toward Olivia and said, "Hello again, ma'am. I hope everything's all right. I'm Will Stanton and this here is my brother, Joe. That was some altercation earlier."

Olivia took in a deep breath. She hadn't wanted to mention anything to Suzanne and Sadie about Walker and the inventory, but knew she'd have to as they both turned to her, their eyes wide and curious.

She turned quickly toward the blacksmiths. "It's very nice to meet you. Olivia Blanchard. Thank you very much for your concern, but it really was nothing."

She shook their hands in turn and raised her lashes to meet the dark, deep eyes of Joe.

"Nothing?" Joe asked as his eyebrows rose.

Will looked puzzled and turned toward his brother. "I hope you're all right. I suppose it didn't hurt that you had your shotgun with you."

Suzanne's hand flew to her chest in alarm. "Olivia, did this have anything to do with Jimmy Joe Walker?"

Olivia pulled her hand slowly back from Joe's and sighed. Concern—or was it curiosity—shadowed his face.

She'd rather have not discussed it with Suzanne

and Sadie, but now that the cat was out of the bag, she might as well. "Yes, it did. He's still after the inventory. Says Pa told him he had first choice on every season's inventory."

Suzanne frowned. "I don't believe that's true. We've bought your inventory every year for many. I don't think your father would say that."

Olivia fingered her sleeve and felt the crinkle of the paper that would prove that he'd said no such thing. "No, he wouldn't. It's definitely a misunderstanding, but Walker won't leave it be."

Sadie took a step back, her eyes wide. "That's shocking. I'm sure your father wouldn't have promised him that," she said as she looked from Suzanne to Olivia.

"Yes, it is," Olivia said slowly as she turned toward Joe and Will's stares. Townsfolk couldn't really understand what it was like to live out on the ranch. It was—well, it was just different. Things happened. Things weren't quite so *polite* and she remembered the looks on their faces when she'd pulled out her shotgun. They'd almost blanched, both of them, even though they'd come to her aid.

"I don't want to bore these gentlemen with business," she said quietly to Suzanne.

Suzanne blinked hard and looked from Olivia to the gentleman. "Oh, yes, right. Nice to see you both," she said as she shook their hands and followed Sadie the rest of the way into the restaurant.

When they were seated, she leaned her head toward Olivia. "Olivia, this sounds serious," she said quietly.

"And dangerous," Sadie added as she placed her napkin in her lap.

"Absolutely," Suzanne said, nodding her head vigorously. "And Percy can't possibly be any help to you. He's...well, he's..."

"Yes, he is," Olivia said and laughed. "Not particularly helpful, to say the least. I'm confident, though, that I can fend them off and get your inventory to you in the next few days. All will be well if we can hurry it up."

Sadie waved to the waitress, asking for tea. "Your pork is the best in the territory, Olivia. There won't be any problem with price. Count on the purchase. Suzanne and I will buy all of it, and we'll settle between us who gets what."

Olivia smiled as the twins exchanged a quick glance, their faces troubled but their crystal blue eyes gleaming. She was quite fond of them both, and sometimes even wished she had their blonde curls and town manners. But that wasn't her lot in life. And besides, she loved the solitude of the ranch and it was her aim to make her father proud, no matter what she had to do to honor his memory.

CHAPTER 7

Olivia had thought she might spend the night at the hotel after her lunch with Suzanne and Sadie, but she found herself anxious to get back to the ranch to finalize the sale. They'd settled on a very generous price for her inventory and shortly, she wouldn't have to pinch pennies any longer.

She breathed a sigh of relief that things had worked out so well. With this money, she could take some time and decide what to do...with the ranch and with herself. This butchering was the final one her father had been involved in, and he'd been very clear during his illness that he didn't expect her to stay a hog farmer forever.

As she passed down the rolling hills that lined the

San Pedro River and the horses settled into a rhythm, she thought of her father. He'd been ill for months before he'd passed, and she'd cherished the opportunities they'd had to talk.

One of the things she remembered most vividly was his insistence that she and Percy finish out the slaughter, sell the bacon and hams at the highest price—that they could get from Sadie and Suzanne—and then sell the ranch. Percy hadn't been too happy about that prospect and even though she'd smiled and nodded while her father spoke, she'd had no intention of moving on from the ranch. The Double Barrel Ranch was all she'd ever known, and she couldn't even conceive of doing anything else.

She crossed the river and the terrain changed as she entered the mountains on the west side. The further she traveled from the river bed, lush with cottonwoods during the monsoon season, the drier the climate. The ranch was in a canyon, and she traveled up the road toward it, the landscape changing from deep green by the water to sparser foliage. Cactus dotted the horizon and the cottonwoods disappeared, replaced with mesquite and palo verde trees that could flourish with much less water.

She flicked the reins and peeked from under her bonnet at the sun as it set behind the mountains.

There were few monsoon clouds and she said a silent thanks for a dry trip home.

As the sky darkened and the clouds to the west changed from white to gray to orange, then purple, she closed her eyes and let the horses find their way home, something they'd done hundreds of times. The stars made their appearance slowly, one by one, and she looked forward to her own bed, in her own home. She was anxious for the silence of the ranch. The fair bit of commotion in town had been plenty of interaction for her for a single day.

Darkness settled in, but in the twilight she saw a plume of dust—a wagon pulled by four horses, racing along at a fairly good clip. They must be hurrying to get home before it was completely dark, like she was. She knew everyone in the canyon, and she squinted to see whose wagon it might be traveling at breakneck speed almost in the dark and her stomach clenched when she couldn't make it out. It wasn't familiar to her at all.

Her eyes followed the trail of dust and she shivered as it ended at the entrance of the Double Barrel Ranch, even pluming from inside the gate. She'd left Percy to guard the ranch, but if the racing wagon had been him—which it wouldn't have since everything he did was slow as molasses—it wasn't their wagon.

She broke into a cold sweat as she sat up straight and flicked the reins again, this time a little more firmly, and the horses broke into a gallop, heading toward the ranch. She kept her eye on the disappearing wagon, still trying to make out some distinguishing features. As she approached the tall, iron gates to the ranch she gave up as the wagon disappeared around the base of a hill, heading toward Tombstone.

She passed under the sign that read Double Barrel Ranch and her eyes searched frantically for the ranch house further on up ahead. She figured Percy had lit a lamp by now with more stars in the sky than twilight, and she looked for it beyond the cactus and mesquite trees lining the drive.

As she rounded the bend, the sight of orange flames licking the sky turned her stomach. No. No, it wasn't possible. Percy was home. Percy was looking after things. Percy...

Where was Percy? She urged the horses faster toward the house and held her breath. On the road home, her eyes had grown accustomed to the darkness and the brightness of the flame almost blinded her. She just headed for the fire—and the house.

In the darkness, it appeared that the house was ablaze and flames shot high in the sky. It wasn't until she had almost reached the fire that she realized it was the smokehouse—not her home—that was turning to ashes right in front of her very eyes.

CHAPTER 8

Joe actually was interested in anything and everything his brother had to say and always had been. Especially now—at least he'd wanted to hear about the trip, but he seemed to be having some difficulty remembering all of it as he sat down to supper with his mother. After closing the shop for the day, he'd headed home and quickly heated up some ham and bean soup that he'd made prior and cornbread to go with it. It was all he had time for as his mother would be waiting for supper.

It wasn't as if he hadn't been paying attention at his lunch with Will—he had—and he was truly happy for Will and his new bride, Carol. And he'd even been excited to hear about Will's training in silversmithing and thought it would be a good addition to the shop. People with money streamed into Tombstone daily as the mines grew and became more profitable. There was plenty of money floating around to spend on the more expensive artistic baubles that these people seemed to covet. In fact, with several other blacksmiths in town and a swelling population that walked to work in the mines, Joe had found himself not all that busy lately.

It seemed like a good business direction for him and Will to go in but he wasn't at all sure he wanted to share that with his mother. It wasn't as if he had to hide it from her as she was much too proud to ask *directly* about Will and Carol, although it was pretty plain to Joe that it was killing her not to.

"So your brother has returned from Chicago?" she asked after at least ten minutes, the only sound in that time the clinking of their spoons in the soup bowls.

"Yes, he has," Joe said as he reached for another piece of cornbread.

He felt his mother's glare settle on him as he finished his beans and wiped his hands on his napkin. He'd learned long ago that she expected him to volunteer information—but it never ended well when he did, so he opted against it now.

The ticking of the clock seemed even louder still as the silence stretched on. His spoon dropped into his bowl as he finished the last of his soup. He folded his napkin, placing it on the table as he stood and reached for his mother's empty bowl.

"Thank you," his mother said as she dabbed at the corners of her mouth, a pinky finger raised.

"You're welcome," he replied as he stacked the bowls and reached for the soup pot. Well, what passed for soup—the best he could do. At least she had the decency not to comment on his cooking as he couldn't remember a time she'd cooked since his pa died. That was left to him and Will, and now with Will gone—well, just him.

She folded her napkin and laid it in front of her, resting her hands on top of it. Sitting back in her chair, she cleared her throat.

"Joseph, I have something I want to talk to you about."

For a moment, the soup bowl in his hand stopped mid-air as he closed his eyes and gathered himself. If she wanted to know about Will and Carol, she'd just have to ask him outright—and it looked like she was going to do just that. He hoped, at least, that they wouldn't get into a row about it, and she would keep her feelings about Carol to herself.

He set the soup pot and bowls on the table and sat down again, crossing his arms over his chest.

"If this is about Will and Carol, I think you should talk to them yourself," he said slowly as he turned toward his mother. After the way she'd treated them so shabbily—refusing, even, to attend their wedding—he wasn't about to make anything easier for her. If she wanted to know, she could thaw her heart and ask them on her own.

She squinted at him and pursed her lips. She clasped her hands together more tightly and annoyance flashed across her face.

Joe tried not to smile. He'd never taken pleasure in seeing her uncomfortable, but her behavior with Will had been extreme, even for her. Since she'd been spending even more time with her sister, the Widow Samson, it had gotten almost unbearable.

"It's not about them. Will has made his feelings known, Joseph, and it's been a horrid time of grief for me. For him to have chosen that...that..."

"Stop right there. Carol may not be able to walk, but she's the sweetest, kindest and I might venture to add smartest young lady I've ever met. She and Will are very much in love, and—"

His mother looked away and waved her hand in Joe's direction. "You can stop right now, Joseph. I counseled Will the best I could, that no good would come of helping the downtrodden. It will be the end of him, just like your father. The subject at hand is not them. Besides, things will be fine as soon as you're married. They won't matter at all. You and your wife will bring me grandchildren, and all will be in order."

Grandchildren? Joe's eyebrows rose and he sat up in his chair, leaning his elbows on the table. He looked around the small dining room, confused. Its barren walls were devoid of any family pictures at all, and mementos marking his and Will's childhood were notably absent. His mother hadn't seemed to enjoy being a mother much, and he was confused that the thought of being a grandmother had even crossed her mind.

"I'm in no hurry, Ma, you know that," he said slowly, wondering what she was after. What was the hurry for him to get married? Sadie and Suzanne had brought it up earlier, also, and then there'd been that woman at dinner the other night. What had been her name? He couldn't remember, but he had no trouble remembering the screechy pitch of her voice—and hoped to never hear it again.

"Jasmine was quite taken with you the other night, Joseph. Dorothy told me herself. She thinks you're quite interesting, and doesn't at all seem to mind that you work in the blacksmith shop. You *are* able to clean up nicely, when need be."

Jasmine. That was her name. In his memory, he'd named her Screechy, and that's how he'd described her and the disaster that was dinner with her and their cousins to Will earlier. Never once had the idea entered his mind that his mother might take this further, as he'd made it quite clear he couldn't wait for the evening to end.

"Ma, I have absolutely no interest in that woman—as a suitor or in any other way imaginable."

His mother looked at him over her spectacles with an expression he was quite familiar with—the one that told him it wasn't his choice, that he would be doing as expected and no discussion would be tolerated. He and Will were pretty quiet, generally, and they'd opted against arguing with her for the most part since their father died but this—marriage? He had to have a say in that, didn't he?

"I'm sorry for that, Joseph, but it's really not relevant. Your aunt and I have taken inventory of the eligible young ladies in Tombstone—and as you know, there are not many, especially as a few of them are your cousins—and this arrival from New Orleans at this time is quite precipitous. She is amenable, and we can have a wedding as quickly as possible."

Joe started to speak, his mouth opening at which point he'd expected words to come out—but none did. As the clock ticked behind him, it occurred to him slowly that she was not jesting.

"Ma, I don't understand what the rush is. I'll find someone. Someone I love, just like Will did."

His mother stiffened, her eyes icy as she turned to him. "And that is the problem. I cannot accept another love match at the risk of having yet another defective daughter-in-law who is unable to take care of my son, let alone having children of her own. Why, it's unthinkable," she said as she rested her hand on her heart.

Joe stood quickly, his chair scraping loudly on the wooden floor of the dining room. He reached for the soup pot and bowls and glanced at his mother before he turned toward the kitchen.

He shook his head slowly. "I'm pleased Pa isn't here to witness those words spoken about Carol, and I don't want to hear it."

"Fine. We won't talk about Will and Carol, but your aunt and I have decided that it's best for you to wed Jasmine. It's your duty as the oldest son to carry on your father's lineage, and Jasmine is the perfect candidate. After what Will has done, we need someone with decency in the family and—"

Joe let the kitchen door swing closed behind him in hopes that he'd have to hear no more of this nonsense. He covered the soup and placed it back in the icebox, his mind jumbled with thoughts of marrying a woman he didn't even know, and not one of his own choosing.

He reached for his coat on the peg by the door and grabbed his hat. It was still light enough to walk back to the shop, and maybe he could make some sense of this there.

As he shoved his hands in his pockets, he felt a paper crinkle. He remembered that Suzanne had shoved something in his hand as he'd left the restaurant but he'd been busy saying goodbye to Will and hadn't taken a look at it.

He unfolded the papers and frowned. The pamphlet was titled *The Grooms' Gazette* and he flipped through the pages, skimming over advertisements from men searching for brides.

The paper crinkled loudly as he placed it back in his pocket. With a swift glance back at the kitchen door, he stepped out, wondering if it might be the only way he could choose his own wife. Even though it would be someone he hadn't met before, he could correspond, exchange letters and maybe see if it was a good match for him. Maybe that would silence his mother—and keep Screechy Jasmine away from him.

CHAPTER 9

Olivia, oblivious to the stares of the people she passed as she guided the buggy down Allen Street, glanced at her hands—covered in soot. The stench of the fire clung to her hair no matter how much she shook her head. She hoped the hotel she had only one night's worth of money to stay in included a bath.

Her best—now her only—dress was covered as well, and the yellow flowers had turned to black smudges some time during the course of the night before she'd given up any further attempts at putting out the fire.

She couldn't stop the memory from replaying in her head, over and over, the entire time it had taken her to ride back into Tombstone. At first, she'd tried emptying the rain barrels, one bucket at a time, doing her best not to curse at the darkness that prevented any of her faraway neighbors from seeing the smoke and coming to help. The fire had been raging when she'd arrived, and no amount of water —certainly not a measly bucket at a time—had squelched the flames even a bit.

When the rain barrels were empty, she'd tried to pump buckets full of water as fast as she could, but still couldn't get ahead of the flames. She'd tried to pump even faster when she spotted the sparks floating over to the house, but even as she gave up on the smokehouse and turned her attention to the flickering embers that settled on the roof of her home, she couldn't pump fast enough.

The realization that she couldn't stay ahead of the flames bolted through her bones, and she ran through the house, one room at a time, throwing things out the front door at the base of the lone oak tree beyond the porch. She hoped it was far enough away and that it wouldn't burn, too. She grabbed what she could, staying one step ahead of the flames as the roof caught, covering her mouth with a wet handkerchief as she coughed. There wasn't any time to decide what to take, and her eyes darted from framed pictures to her mother's crockery.

Panic finally seized her as the kitchen curtains went up in flame, the floral fabric almost melting in the heat. The sight of her mother sewing those very curtains before she died flitted in her mind's eye and she had to turn away. She bolted to her bedroom and grabbed what she could and rushed to her parents' room. She stopped for a moment and reached for the picture of her parents that her father had kept by his bedside for years and wiped away a smudge.

The window of the bedroom she'd just left shattered and she was jolted back into the moment. She threw what things she could find onto her father's bed and wrapped them in the blanket, dragging them outside and under the tree. She turned inside once more, but flames peeked out of the front door and she had to accept she was finished. The house would be no more.

She'd left the horses tied to a tree out by the gate so they wouldn't bolt and had immediately started to put out the fire. Her heart broke as they whinnied, watching the fire engulf the house as she dropped the blanket and slowly backed away. It took all the courage she could muster to admit defeat. She tasted the salt of her own tears that streamed down her face as she finally turned away and headed toward the horses.

She'd shouted desperately for Percy, hoping to find some help, but she'd been met with silence. His bunk in the barn near the smokehouse hadn't yet been engulfed in flames by the time she'd gotten there, and she certainly hoped he'd not been harmed. By the light of the flames, she hadn't seen anything that would tell her otherwise and gave thanks that she hadn't found his body. Not yet, anyway.

She'd groaned at the thought, but shook her head. Her father would never have let this happen. How *had* it happened?

She carried the last bucket of water she'd pumped to the horses and slumped to the ground as they drank, her back to the house as it disappeared in flames. Exhausted, she stretched out on the ground, hesitating a moment before she realized that the dirt she was lying on couldn't make her dress any worse than it was.

She looked up at the stars and took in a deep breath. They twinkled brightly, seemingly oblivious that her entire world was going up in flames. The moon shined brightly, but the stars still mocked her efforts at saving her home, and she couldn't stop the despair that rose from deep in her soul.

"I'm sorry, Pa. I'm so sorry," she whispered between sobs before the sorrow overtook her, and she'd cried herself to sleep.

CHAPTER 10

Joe slept fitfully that night, wondering what to say in his ad in *The Grooms' Gazette*. Looking for a mail order bride wasn't something he'd even considered yesterday—or even heard much about, really—but Sadie's words had stuck with him, rolling over in his mind.

And after supper, he knew his mother was set on his marrying screechy Jasmine or someone just like her and wouldn't take no for an answer. This mail order bride idea just might be the thing to save him if he could manage marrying someone he'd never met. The way Sadie had described it, he'd have a chance to get to know about some ladies and have his choice of who he'd like to correspond with. Nice and slow, that sounded good. He could correspond for a while to see if it was a good match before he committed to anything, anyway. And when he announced it to his mother, she'd be on to another project. He hoped so, anyway.

He washed up and dressed for his day at the blacksmith shop. Will would be coming in eventually, but he wanted to get there early and clean up before his brother arrived. They both liked things in order and Joe wanted Will to feel welcome and comfortable as they discussed the new venture Will had been in Chicago learning about, silversmithing. He'd written about that in the letter he'd penned when he woke up, the one that he'd give to Suzanne as soon as the mercantile opened, and hoped Will would look it over first, as well.

As was customary for him these days, he didn't slow down as he reached the bottom of the stairs, reached for his hat and said, "Goodbye, Ma," with his hand already on the door latch. He might have even walked a little more quickly this morning, hoping he wouldn't have any repeat of the previous evening's discussion, especially before he could implement his plan.

The letter safely in his pocket, Joe unlocked the shop and the neighboring livery where they kept horses if needed while people were in town. Joe pulled his pocket watch from his vest and glanced at the time. Too early for Luke to be in, but they wouldn't likely have any customers for a bit yet. The stable hand had plenty of time to get to work.

Joe closed the gate to the livery and turned toward the shop next door, hoping to brew a quick pot of coffee before starting for the day. He'd take a break later and head to the mercantile, maybe grabbing a pastry from Sadie or a meat pie when his stomach started to grumble. But for now, he'd straighten up the shop and get ready for Will.

Joe slipped the key into the lock and turned it, throwing the door open.

"You open for business over at the livery?" a woman's voice said as he stepped inside the door. He thought it sounded familiar, but as he turned he couldn't imagine where he'd ever seen this woman before. He took off his hat and his eyebrows rose, but he did his best to hide any other expression.

"Uh, the stable hand hasn't quite arrived yet," Joe said after he'd cleared his throat. He checked his pocket watch—Luke wasn't expected until after three in the afternoon as he'd asked for some time off today.

The woman in the buggy before him was covered

head to toe in soot, but her green eyes pierced him through the black as she met his gaze.

"I'm not sure I have time to wait. I think I might need a bath," she said as she looked down at her hands.

"That may be," Joe said as he hung his hat on the hook just inside the door and turned back to the lady. "I was just about to make some coffee if you'd like to wait a few minutes, see if he arrives."

The lady sighed and tried to brush some of the soot off her dress, but it didn't move. "You sure you want me inside your shop in this state?"

Joe laughed. "I probably have enough soot in there to match you. Come on in."

Joe took her hand and helped her down from the buggy. Her hand was warm and surprisingly soft, and he bit his tongue rather than ask her what had happened. His mother talked enough for the entire family, and since his pa had died, he and his brother had been pretty quiet. Safer that way—in his house at least.

He gestured to the client chair he kept by his desk as he pumped water into the coffee pot, stoked the fire and set it on the stove. He reached for a clean cloth as the lady settled in the chair. He watched her from the corner of his eye as she looked up and down Allen Street. Even through the soot, he could see she had lovely skin, and her hair was silky even though it was covered in grime—long brown locks in a braid.

He soaked the cloth in the water that was a little warmer now and wrung it out over the water barrel he used to cool hot steel. She took it gently from him when he held it out to her, her eyes offering gratitude along with sadness.

She coughed for a bit, and as she wiped the soot from her face, he realized that it was the young lady he'd met the previous day at the Occidental.

"Oh," he said, startled. "Miss Blanchard. I didn't recognize you, what with the..."

"That bad?" she asked as she wiped the soot from her eyes.

He'd thought she looked somehow familiar—her soft, green eyes had struck him once again—but he truly hadn't recognized her from the day before. He noticed now that she was wearing the same dress but it bore little resemblance to the way he remembered it. He'd watched her leave the Occidental and recalled thinking how lovely she was. What could possibly have happened to her since that time?

Would it have had anything to do with the altercation he'd witnessed?

"Are you all right, miss?" he asked when he couldn't bear his curiosity any longer.

She glanced down at the black rag that had been clean and white when she'd started wiping her face. He took it from her and rinsed it again. She reached for it again gratefully and began wiping her hands.

"I haven't even a mirror left to my name."

He couldn't help thinking that she wouldn't want to see one at this particular moment, but opted not to mention it.

"What happened, if you don't mind my asking?" he asked softly as he sat back in his chair.

She handed the rag back to him, and as his hand brushed against hers, his heart tugged at the sadness in her eyes. He felt the familiar pull—that his mother regularly urged him to resist—to help her.

"I'm not exactly sure what happened, to be honest," she said as she fiddled with the reticule she held. "I returned home to my family's ranch last night after my day in town to find it ablaze. I tried everything I could to save it but..."

Her voice trailed off as she shook the bag in her hand and several coins jingled. Not many, he could tell.

"What a tragedy," he said, as it was all he could think of.

"Yes, quite. The house went up in flames as well as the smokehouse. A year's worth of inventory and income, gone."

"I'm so sorry." Joe reached for her hand out of instinct as she lowered her head, a sob escaping her as he did. "Was anyone injured?"

She caught her breath and looked into his deep, brown eyes.

"Injured? Oh, no. My parents passed a while back, and I couldn't find Percy. I don't know if he's still there and I just didn't find him...I truly don't know."

"Percy?" Joe asked, curious to know if that was her husband—and surprised that he wanted to know.

"Our ranch hand. He's a little older, and I hope—well, I hope he wasn't..."

"Oh, I see," Joe said as he released her hand and stood to pour her some coffee. He wasn't sure what to say—not sure how he could help her short of offering to look for Percy, whom he did not know. He didn't know the young lady, really, either.

He held a cup of coffee toward her, unsure what

to do next. It was clear she had little money and he wasn't sure she had much of a plan.

She looked at the coffee and held up her hands. "I really should be going. Do you think your stable hand will be here soon? I need to figure out what to do. If I even have any options."

Joe set down the coffee and looked out the window. Without hesitation, he said, "I'll take care of the buggy. You go ahead. It can stay here as long as you need."

Her shoulders softened as she stood and she offered a weak smile. She opened her reticule and reached inside.

Joe held up his hands and shook his head. "No, please, I've no need of your money. Please, let me help in this small way."

"Oh, no, I couldn't impose..."

"No imposition," he said quickly and reached to open the door for her. He found himself wanting to follow, to see how she did, or what she did, but he bid her good luck and closed the door behind her. He watched as she walked up Allen Street slowly, and didn't turn away until she was safely inside the mercantile. He wondered what she'd think when she finally reached a mirror, the cloth having done an inadequate job of clearing the soot, but he somehow had the sense that she'd be able to take care of herself...and reminded himself that if his mother was there, she'd tell him to mind his own business, and that no good ever came of helping.

CHAPTER 11

"My goodness. What happened to you? You look a fright!" Suzanne exclaimed when she opened the door of the mercantile to let Olivia in. She'd stood on the boardwalk for a few moments before she'd squared her shoulders and decided to knock. She had to tell Suzanne about the inventory as soon as possible and the soot could wait, as far as she was concerned. She was too exhausted to care much about what she looked like, but judging by Suzanne's reaction, and the earlier reaction of the blacksmith, she must look horrible.

Olivia sat down in the chair Suzanne pulled her toward and let her face fall in her hands.

"Suzanne, it's horrible. The ranch has burned, and all the inventory and Percy is—well, I don't know where Percy is and it's all gone. All of it." The words tumbled out and Olivia didn't stop until she realized Suzanne hadn't spoken. She looked up to see Suzanne leave the mercantile to return seconds later with Sadie in tow.

Sadie's hand flew to her mouth at the sight of Olivia, and she rushed over and wrapped her in her arms, soot and all. Olivia's heart burst and she sobbed into Sadie's shoulder, feeling the comforting hands of the twins stroking her hair.

When she caught her breath, she sat up straight. She looked from one twin to the other, their faces shadowed with concern. "I don't know what to do."

An uncomfortable silence fell and Olivia sniffled, wiping at her face with the handkerchief Suzanne had given her. It was black when she pulled it away and she shook her head.

"I really just came to explain that I don't have any of the inventory we spoke about yesterday. It was nowhere that I could see—none left at all. It must have all burned before I got home," she said slowly, standing and pacing on the heavy wooden planks of the floor.

"Olivia, don't you worry about that. We'll find a solution," Sadie said as she glanced at Suzanne. "We

THE BLACKSMITH'S MAIL ORDER BRIDE

have lots of suppliers to choose from. We just like yours best."

Olivia frowned. "I know you do. And I don't mean to sound selfish, but I have no other income. I was counting on my sale to you to carry me through the winter. Now I have nothing at all. Not even enough money to stay at the hotel but for a night."

"Oh, dear," Sadie said as her eyebrows furrowed. "We can worry about a better plan after you get cleaned up. But for now, I'd love it if you came to stay with me. Tripp and I have room."

"I couldn't possibly impose," Olivia said as she sat back down. "I just need a good night's sleep. I'm sure I'll come up with something."

"Olivia, don't be silly. We can talk more about this later at supper. Let's get you over to Sadie's so you can get some rest. I don't suppose you slept much, and it was a long ride into town."

Suzanne and Sadie waited while Olivia tried to sort out what to do. There was no ranch to go back to, and while she hated to impose her troubles on anyone else, sincerity and concern radiated from both of the twins.

"I...I believe I must accept your kind offer. But only for a short while, until I can sort this out."

Sadie breathed a sigh of relief as she reached for

Olivia's hand. "Come, let's go now. I'm not needed tonight at the Occidental. We'll have time to get you a bath, and we can talk about it more over supper."

Olivia struggled to put one foot in front of the other as she followed Sadie, almost blindly. It was early evening by the time they arrived, and her fingers clung to the oak bannister to help her up to the room Sadie indicated she'd stay in. Her eyes were as heavy as lead and she struggled to smile, thanking Sadie for her kindness before she plopped onto the bed.

She looked down at her dress, that had once been covered with bright yellow flowers. It was completely black, now. She thought she shouldn't even be sitting on a bed covered in so much soot, but couldn't muster the energy to stand. She could find no words and lifted her lashes toward Sadie as best she could, desperately trying to make sense of what had happened in such a short time.

"Sadie, I'm sorry," she said softly.

Sadie rested her hand on Olivia's shoulder and brushed back some of her curls that had fallen across her face. "Don't worry, Olivia. Everything will turn out all right. You'll see."

The gesture and Sadie's kind words brought tears to her eyes, and she laid back on the soft bed, not even enough energy to remove her dress, as Sadie closed the door gently behind her.

She leaned back on the bed and said a prayer of thanks for the roof over her head—even if it wasn't her own. Before she could even remove her shoes, her eyes closed to merciful darkness and she fell fast asleep.

CHAPTER 12

Olivia sat bolt upright as the grandfather clock downstairs struck seven. Panic shot through her as she looked down at her dress. If she didn't hurry, she'd miss supper, and she'd wanted to help. How could she have slept so long?

She groaned as she wiggled her toes—she hadn't even taken off her filthy boots. How could she have been so tired to not even do that?

The empty room was lovely—she hadn't even noticed when they'd arrived, she'd been so tired. A porcelain washbasin and pitcher stood on the white, marble top of the oak vanity. It was very similar to her room at home, and she shook her head, reminding herself that she had no home. This was Sadie's, and she'd kindly offered to share.

Supper would be soon, but she didn't have time to wash up. Besides, she needed much more than just to rinse her face. She rushed to the door and down the stairs. She would find Sadie and see if she had time to clean up before supper. Shoot, she didn't even have a dress to change into. Nothing at all.

Halfway down the stairs, her stomach rumbled at the delicious aroma of coffee and bread. Sadie must have been working all afternoon, all on her own, and with a baby on the way, to boot. Heat crept into Olivia's cheeks as she quickly pulled her hair back and swung open the door to the kitchen.

She'd been fully prepared to apologize and help with supper, but the kitchen was empty. A warm pot of coffee sat on the wood stove and a warm loaf of bread graced the table, a jar of marmalade set to the side.

Where could everyone be? She paced for a moment, wondering if they'd been tied up at the restaurant or the mercantile. She crossed over to the back door and stepped out onto the small porch, breathing deeply of the fresh, cool air. She looked left and right and squinted at the sun as it sat atop the mountains to the east. East? She spun on the porch to get her bearings. Yes, that certainly was east and if it was, then it was—morning?

Oh, goodness, I slept all night!

Her stomach knotted as she rushed back through the house and grabbed her bonnet. She must apologize. Sadie and Suzanne had wanted to talk to her more about the inventory, and the *Grooms' Gazette* and a host of other things and she'd slept right through the evening.

She shook her head as she climbed the steps to the mercantile. The sign still said, "Closed," but she knocked anyway, needing to apologize, needing to—well, talk to someone.

"Olivia!" Suzanne said as she came from around the counter of the mercantile, wiping her hands on her apron. "I'm so glad you're here. We didn't have the heart to wake you last night, you were dead to the world. You look—well, a little more rested, if not much cleaner." She smiled as she held her hand to Olivia's cheek. "How do you feel?"

Heat crept into Olivia's cheeks as she looked down at her dress.

"Like I've been run over by a herd of cattle," Olivia said as she returned Suzanne's smile.

Suzanne's blue eyes twinkled as she squeezed Olivia's hand. "Let me run and get Sadie. She's been anxious to talk with you."

Olivia wandered the aisles of the mercantile as

she waited. She took in a deep breath as she lifted her chin. She'd decided on the way over to the mercantile that she may as well make the best of things.

Suzanne cleared her throat as she and Sadie approached the counter. Sadie smiled and nodded at Suzanne as she and leaned back against the counter. "Olivia, I know it was just yesterday, but things have changed quite a bit since then for you, to say the least. Sadie and I have discussed this, and we think you should consider a change of even greater magnitude. I know it seems sudden, but you do know that several of the ladies in town—including Sadie—have thrown in their lot and become mail order brides."

Olivia did know about that—some of the Archer girls had done the same as Sadie and they all seemed to be happy. But that was an option that hadn't even crossed her mind before now.

"I know it seems sudden, but have you considered looking at some of the advertisements for a mail order bride in *The Grooms' Gazette*? I was looking at it last night after you left and there are quite a few interesting advertisements," Sadie said as she folded her hands over her apron.

Suzanne turned and reached behind the counter,

pulling out what looked to Olivia like a newspaper, or some sort of magazine.

She'd never even entertained the notion of something so drastic. The day before yesterday, her biggest problem had been what to do with all the money she'd have when she sold the inventory, and planning for next year. But now—who was she to discount anything at all?

Olivia stood and reached for the newspaper. Suzanne smiled and nodded at Sadie. "We would be happy to help in any way we can."

"Tripp and I have been very happy, Olivia, and I moved here all the way from Chicago to meet him," Sadie said as she rubbed her belly that seemed big enough to burst. "And the baby is due soon. We're a family."

Olivia managed a smile as she opened the newspaper. Sadie did seem very happy, and she'd heard that she and Susan had had some other successes. But the thought...what would her pa think? Her ma? Grief washed over her as she remembered that they were both gone. They wouldn't know anything about it except from Heaven. She truly was on her own now, with even Percy gone.

"I wouldn't even know where to begin," Olivia

said after a few moments of weighing her very few options. She could try to sell the property at the ranch, but it wasn't as if they had cultivated it as farmland. They'd been hog farmers ever since she was a little girl, and the hogs and the house were gone, so there wasn't going to be much demand for the Double Barrel Ranch. And she'd sell it to Jimmy Joe Walker over her dead body.

She'd thought about what jobs she could get, but all of her skills were better suited for a farm—shooting, hunting, fixing guns, repairing wagon wheels, shoeing horses, slaughtering hogs...not things that were helpful for a lady to get a job in a town.

A rap sounded on the door and Olivia jumped.

"I'd better open up," Suzanne said as she patted Olivia's shoulder and exchanged a worried glance with Sadie.

Suzanne glanced at the clock and jumped up. She headed over to the sign at the window and turned it to "Open", unlocking the door and crossing back to Sadie and Olivia.

The bells of the door jingled. "Is the young lady all right?" a rich, deep voice said from the door. The ladies looked up, and Olivia sighed at the sight of the first person to help her—Joe, the blacksmith.

"We've all had quite a fright, but she seems to be physically sound," Suzanne said as she walked over to Joe, pulling him toward the counter by his elbow. "I didn't realize it was you. Come on in, Joe. I'll be with you in a moment."

Olivia glanced back down at the paper in her hands as Suzanne said, "Like I said, Sadie and I will help you. We can sit and go through the advertisements together and see what appeals to you. You can stay at Sadie's until you've found a suitable...well, a suitable suitor," she said with a broad smile as she hugged Olivia.

"Oh, my. I don't know," Olivia said as she glanced from one identical twin to the other. "I'm not sure I'd fit in as someone's wife. I'm not very good at those wifely kinds of things." The thought of how she'd taken care of the ranch, and her father—even her mother as she'd died slowly—and she couldn't stop the flow of tears. Panic rushed through her suddenly, and she fought to catch her breath.

Suzanne stroked her hair, and her breath began to slow as she wiped her eyes.

"Of course you are. You are a fine cook, and you've kept a house for years. You just have no experience with having a man in it—Percy doesn't count

—and that part's easy to learn," Sadie said with a smile.

She knew they were trying to help, and she racked her brain for a moment for some means to support herself. Not finding any solutions, she was about to say yes when the blacksmith, who she'd completely forgotten was in the room, cleared his throat.

She looked up at him, his deep brown eyes trained on her. He'd been the first person to help her the day before. He'd seemed just as quiet then as now, and she remembered that he'd seemed a little taken aback during her altercation with Walker.

He had a piece of paper in his hand, and their eyes met as he handed it to Suzanne.

Suzanne unfolded the paper carefully and her eyes grew wide as she read whatever was on it. She looked up from the paper at Joe questioningly as she handed the document to her sister.

Sadie skimmed the paper quickly and smiled, folding it and placing it back in Joe's hand. She clapped once and squeezed her sister's hand as the door bells rang but no one looked toward the door. All eyes were on Joe. Including Olivia's, but she didn't quite understand why.

THE BLACKSMITH'S MAIL ORDER BRIDE

"What do you think, Mr. Stanton?" Suzanne asked, very formally in Olivia's opinion.

Joe twisted his hat in his hands and nodded at Suzanne, who grabbed her sister's hand again. Both twins' smiles spread from ear to ear.

"Go ahead, then," Suzanne urged as Sadie's hand flew to her mouth and her eyes grew even wider.

The blacksmith ran a hand through his dark, wavy hair and held his hat over his chest. He blew out a breath and turned toward Olivia as he shoved the mysterious paper back in his pocket.

"Miss Blanchard, it appears that you are in need of a husband, and I'm in need of a wife. Would you do me the honor of becoming mine? I can promise you a safe and secure home. I guess we'll have to see what happens from there."

Olivia gasped and held her hand over her heart. She really looked at him, as if for the first time. He was taller than her by a head, and he was very handsome—but her eyes were trained on his. The deep brown pulled her in, and the smile wrinkles around them—well, she made up her mind.

A bead of sweat appeared on his forehead and she turned and looked at both Sadie and Suzanne. They both grinned and nodded, and as her life had been completely upended in the space of a single day, she decided to trust them, her longtime friends, and she wasn't sure if she surprised all of them, but she sure surprised herself when she said, "Well, yes. I suppose I will. Thank you for asking."

CHAPTER 13

Joe couldn't believe his own ears. Or his eyes. Had he really just asked a woman he barely knew—one covered in soot from head to toe—to marry him? Granted, he'd not been able to think of much else since he'd met her. He'd fought the urge to check on her several times, but seeing her now—well, he'd been quite relieved to see she was all right.

He'd sat silently by while she told her tale of woe, and a doozy it was. She'd lost everything—her ranch, her home, her father fairly recently, and all of her inventory that was to carry her for a year. Hard work that was, too, hog farming.

His mother's voice had crossed his mind once or

twice as she'd told her tale and he'd fought the urge to help.

"Joseph, remember what happened to your father. There's no good in helping. Just keep to yourself and mind your own business," she said in his memory.

But this woman, Olivia, was in dire straights, with nothing to her name and no prospects. When Sadie and Suzanne had suggested she set out to be a mail order bride, his hand had crept into his pocket. He fiddled with the advertisement he'd written and had planned to give to Suzanne to send to the newspaper, and the thought that here was a girl that he at least knew right in front of him considering answering an ad something like the one he held at that very moment.

He knew he wanted to steer his mother away from what would no doubt be a disastrous union if she had the opportunity to plan it, and at least Olivia was someone he'd met and found interesting—if interesting was the right word. The thought grew as she spoke, and when both Suzanne and Sadie had nodded, guessing his plan, it just sort of happened.

And now she'd accepted. He glanced over at Suzanne, hoping for some direction, as this was uncharted territory for him. And for Olivia, too, he was certain.

"Now what do we do?" he said as the bells to the door jingled.

Suzanne kept her attention on Olivia. "You're sure you want to do this, Olivia?" she asked, her eyebrows raised.

"I think...yes, yes, I am sure," Olivia said as her cheeks flushed. Sadie hugged Olivia once again and held her shoulders, standing back. "We'll have to get you cleaned up so he can see the beauty he's getting," she whispered in Olivia's ear during the hug.

"Oh!" Olivia cried.

"How about this Sunday?" Suzanne asked as she turned to Joe. "Might as well get on with it."

"Get on with what?" a tall, large woman asked as she stepped directly in front of Joe.

Joe groaned as he took a step back. Of all the luck. Why did his aunt have to turn up now? Here, of all places?

He took a deep breath and said, "Olivia, please meet my aunt, Mrs. Samson. She's my mother's sister."

Olivia stepped forward and smiled, holding out her hand to her future relative.

The older woman recoiled, her gloved hand on

her chest as she gasped. "Young lady, you are filthy. I wouldn't dream of shaking your hand."

Suzanne had an odd expression on her face as she leaned back against the counter and folded her hands in front of her. "Mrs. Samson, Olivia is Joe's fiancée. He's just asked her to marry him."

The widow blanched as she blinked quickly, looking at each of the four in turn. She settled on Joseph and looped her arm through his. "Oh, you silly girls. I know a joke when I hear one," she said before her laughter filled the room.

Sadie moved over to stand beside Olivia, looping her own arm through her friend's. "It's not a joke, Mrs. Samson. We all are very pleased."

Joe stiffened as all eyes turned on him. Seemed like now was the time to come clean. They'd all hear about it at some point anyway, so it might as well be now.

"Yes, Aunt Dorothy, Olivia has agreed to marry me. I believe I'm a very fortunate man."

His aunt sputtered and coughed as she braced herself against the counter. When she'd caught her breath, she said, "That is not possible. It cannot be—will not be permitted. What about Jasmine? She has made plans—"

"That is no fault of mine," Joe interrupted as he

squared his shoulders. "You and my mother had no right to promise her anything, particularly in relation to my intentions. I've made my mind up, and I have acted on it. Olivia and I will be wed this Sunday."

The older lady tucked a strand of her gray hair back into her bun and pulled on her gloves. She glowered at Joe, and he remembered what that had felt like his whole life. She was as sour as his mother, but worse.

He felt almost lighter than he had in years as he stood tall and crossed to stand beside Olivia himself, offering her his arm. His heart warmed as she looked up at him, her deep green eyes uncertain. He covered her hand when she looped her arm through his and winked at her.

"I—does your mother know about this?" she said, her voice low and menacing. "Surely, she won't condone this atrocity."

"I'll thank you to hold your tongue if that's all you have to say, Aunt Dorothy. Olivia and I are to be wed, and what my mother thinks or feels about it has no merit in my mind whatsoever. Of course, I do wish she would approve, but if she doesn't it won't change a thing."

The widow tapped her cane on the floor, almost

hard enough that Joe thought it might go straight through the wooden planks. She narrowed her eyes at him and straightened her hat, her skirts swishing loudly as she headed for the door.

"We'll see about that, young man," she said over her shoulder as sound of the door slamming reverberated through the room.

Joe heard Olivia breathe a heavy sigh and he was sorry that her first introduction to her new family was his aunt. He wasn't at all convinced that she would change her demeanor before or after the wedding, and his stomach roiled at the thought of what would surely be coming soon.

Suzanne looked worriedly at the door as customers filtered in. She turned to Joe and said softly, "You two might want to consider getting married sooner rather than later, before the coming storm develops into a hurricane."

"Yes, that would be wise. It would be better to present this to my mother as a fait accompli," Joe said as he turned toward Olivia. "I'm sorry for her behavior, Olivia. I'd like to say she's not always like that—"

"But she is," Sadie interrupted. "I agree with Suzanne. The sooner the better before you have to face the wrath of your mother."

Joe worried that after all this, Olivia just might change her mind and he wished they could just go ahead and get hitched. His smile widened as he saw Suzanne crossing the mercantile with a young man in tow.

"And I think I have just the solution. Joe, Olivia, you know Pastor Daughtry. Pastor, do you have a few free moments?" she said, and Joe squeezed Olivia's hand, relieved that she squeezed his back.

It would be all right. He would make it so.

CHAPTER 14

"I suppose that's it, then. We're married." Joe's voice floated to Olivia's ears as though through a fog. Everything had happened so quickly—the pastor agreed, Suzanne shoved a flower in her hand, she and Joe said, "I do," and now—well, she was married, all before breakfast.

She still felt like she was in a dream—or nightmare, when she thought of the fire—as she followed Sadie up the porch steps of her home. Olivia hadn't said much, but it had been decided that she'd spend the night at Sadie's house so that she could get cleaned up and Joe could see to arrangements at his house. She'd be moving there tomorrow.

Moving where? She didn't even know. Stapleton?

Stockton? She wasn't even sure she knew Joe's last name, which would now be hers. She'd heard the pastor say it but she couldn't remember. She shook her head, trying to end the buzzing that coursed through her body, and let it all sink in.

"Do you have a bag or anything?" Sadie asked as she gestured for Olivia to enter her parlor. Olivia lifted her skirts to cross the threshold and got a glimpse of her filthy skirt and boots.

"No, I don't. This is all I have," she replied as she unbuttoned her boots and left them outside. She wouldn't make the same mistake twice and fall asleep with her boots on.

Sadie's house was lovely, and quite comfortable. The evening before, she hadn't noticed the white lace curtains, velvet settee and Oriental rug gracing the parlor. Cozy. It was cozy.

A shiver ran through Olivia as she remembered how cozy the ranch house had been—the curtains her mother had made going up in flames in her mind's eye.

"Are you cold?" Sadie said as she led Olivia through the parlor and into the kitchen. She hadn't noticed much about the kitchen earlier, either. She'd never thought about what a chef's kitchen at home would be like, but of course it would be something like this—copper pans hung on the ceiling of all types and sizes, spices lining one of the counters, the wonderful aroma of warm bread.

Before Olivia could answer, her stomach grumbled and her hand flew to her waist. She couldn't remember the last time she'd eaten—oh, yes, she'd been at the restaurant two days ago and not eaten since. She hadn't realized it until this very second.

Sadie set the bread and prickly pear jam on the table—Olivia's favorite—and her stomach grumbled again.

"It would appear that you're hungry, and I can imagine why. Tripp will bring home some meat pies from the Occidental later at lunchtime, but for now this and a cup of tea will do you some good."

"You're about to have a baby, Sadie. I can do that myself."

Sadie waved her hand at Olivia. "I wouldn't think of it. I'm fine. If women stopped doing things because they were going to have a baby, nothing would get done, would it?" she said as she put the kettle on the stove, stoked the fire, cut slices of bread, then slathered them with the jam.

All Olivia could do was nod gratefully and sit in the chair Sadie had pulled out for her.

"Besides, the baby isn't due to arrive quite yet. I

know people want me to just sit and wait, but I can't do it." Sadie reached out onto the back porch for a bucket and set it under the water pump.

"I suppose it might be a little difficult when you're accustomed to working so much," Olivia said as she washed her hands in the kitchen sink.

"So, Olivia, it seems you're a married woman," Sadie said softly as she sat down beside Olivia, setting warm tea in front of her.

Olivia wasn't quite sure what to say, and Sadie waited patiently, stirring a spoonful of sugar into her tea.

The cream she'd poured into her own tea swirled as she stirred it slowly, her shoulders heavy as she thought about what she'd done. It had all happened so quickly that there hadn't really been time to think.

Until now.

She looked up slowly at Sadie and tears pricked her eyes. Sadie sighed and reached for Olivia's hand. The kindness made Olivia's breath hitch in her throat before the sob came, and she pulled her hand back and covered her eyes. It was an odd sensation that Olivia was unaccustomed to. She hadn't even had time to wallow in despair. Her life had already changed forever—and for the good, she hoped.

"Olivia, Joe is a fine man. Suzanne and I would never have encouraged you to consider his proposal if we didn't trust that he would be good to you and look after you as you deserve."

Olivia caught her breath and folded her hands in her lap. "I know that, Sadie. I made a quick decision because of that. I trust the two of you. I don't think I would have done it otherwise."

"Good," Sadie said. "I won't lie—his mother will be a bit of a challenge. As will his aunt. But the brothers are wonderful men with a prosperous shop. Joe has a very pretty home on the north side of town, and—well, if we can settle things with his mother..."

"Please tell me what I'm in for. Is she just like his aunt? She was—she didn't seem very happy. Or understanding."

"Understanding? No, I certainly wouldn't say she is. The Widow Samson is well known around town for making things—well, difficult, to say the least. Rose Archer had quite a few run-ins with her, but she and Michael are very happy now. No thanks to the Widow Samson."

"What does she have against people marrying and finding their own happiness?"

Sadie hid her smile behind her hand and her eyes widened.

"The widow lost her husband several years ago. Of undetermined causes, I might add, and she seems never to have recovered. And, of course, Joe lost his father in a terrible accident, and I believe his mother is equally unhappy because of it. But I should let Joe tell you that story," Sadie said. She leaned forward and peered out the kitchen window, holding back the curtains that reminded Olivia of the curtains in her own home—or the home she'd had once.

"Looks like it might rain tonight. I'm terribly sorry it didn't rain the night of the fire. It might have helped."

That thought had occurred to Olivia more than once as she had lain back, watching the stars in the cloudless sky. Tombstone had very unpredictable weather in the summer months, with monsoon rain storms appearing sometimes within minutes. Why couldn't that have happened as she watched the flames die down on their own? It sure would have helped.

Sadie stood up slowly, leaning against the back of the chair to support her weight. She winced a bit, and Olivia stood. "Can I help you?"

Sadie laughed. "No. For all my talk of wanting to

do everything myself, sometimes I get little twinges, but it's all right. I think I'll do better when the baby comes if I stay busy."

"I don't know how you do it."

"You ran an entire ranch by yourself, my dear—Percy aside—so you do know exactly how I do it."

Sadie started to lift the full bucket from the sink, but took in a sharp breath as she did.

Olivia jumped up and took the bucket from her hands, setting it on the floor. "See, that's what I mean. That's too heavy for you, especially right now."

Sadie rubbed her lower back as her other hand rested on her belly. She smiled weakly and said, "Maybe you're right. I probably shouldn't be lifting heavy things at the moment, but I honestly think you should have a bath and a good rest before Joseph arrives for supper."

Olivia turned back to the sink and caught a glimpse of herself in the mirror. She gasped and her hands flew to her hair. She spun quickly, her eyes as big as saucers as she said, "Good gracious. I look like a monster."

She turned back to the window and began to loosen her braids.

Sadie leaned on the table and laughed. "I have to say, I've seen you look much better."

Olivia spun around again, her cheeks bright red. "And Joe *married* me like this."

Her friend's blue eyes twinkled. "Yes, he did. And I have no doubt that he was happy to, Olivia. I believe you two may be surprised at how well you get on."

She quickly began to unbraid her hair. "How can he have any idea what he's gotten himself into?" Olivia asked as a laugh escaped and she smiled widely, her long, dark hair falling unfettered down her back.

"We'll get you back to normal. I haven't worn any of my dresses from before I was with child, and I venture to guess I won't be wearing them any time soon. You're welcome to them, and I'm sure they'll fit you."

Olivia's heart swelled as she hugged her friend. Her life had been upended, and here they were laughing. She felt a little hopeful for the first time since she'd watched the ranch go up in flames and she vowed to do her best as a wife and make things right with Joe's mother. Certainly she couldn't be as sour as his aunt.

She lifted the bucket of water onto the stove. "I

think you were right about that bath, if you don't mind. I don't think I've ever been this filthy, even during slaughtering season. I guess Joe married the dirtiest, most exhausted hog farmer in the world. Good luck to him, I say," she said as both women dissolved into laughter.

CHAPTER 15

Joe closed the door to the blacksmith shop slowly and leaned against it, throwing his hat onto the hook by the door. He stood there for a moment, trying to remember why he'd gone to the mercantile in the first place—a decision that had now changed his life completely.

It seemed like weeks ago, not merely a day, that the young lady covered in soot had sat in this very shop, seemingly in shock, and he'd wanted to help her. Wanted to, but hadn't, really. Not much. She hadn't even had coffee.

He wasn't sure he'd ever know what moved him to make such a bold proposal after he'd seen her. She hadn't even seemed to notice that he was there, such was her grief. And terror. And hopelessness.

It was almost as if he'd been taken back to that day—the day his father lost his life. He'd been so young then, Will even younger—both of them too young to do anything to help.

It was years ago, and yet it was still fresh in his mind as if it had been yesterday. Standing in the mercantile, his heart had been squeezed as it had that day long ago, when he hadn't been able to change the hand of fate. Olivia wept today as his mother had back then, and he'd just been compelled to—act.

He had given in to a moment of trepidation, his mother's voice ringing in his ears. His father had been helping—or trying to—a young miner recently arrived to Tombstone, and it had gotten him killed. Maybe if they hadn't all had guns, maybe if it had just been a fistfight it might have turned out differently. That's certainly what his mother thought and why they'd been forbidden from ever working on or even cleaning guns in the blacksmith shop since they'd taken it over after his father's passing.

But this—this girl's dilemma side by side to his own—this was hardly as dangerous. Foolhardy, possibly. But dangerous? How could it be? It was a wedding, not a duel. At least for now.

As he pushed himself away from the door and reached for his heavy leather apron to start his work day, he wondered if it might be better for him if he *was* armed when he told his mother what he'd done. He would certainly need some defense, judging by the reaction of his aunt. He knew that she'd have told his mother by now, but he also knew she wouldn't come to the shop to confront him. That event would be later in the afternoon when he went home. She'd refused to enter the shop since his father passed, and Joe said a small thanks of gratitude for that fact.

As he rolled the words over in his mind that he'd share with his mother later, he wished his brother were there. He really should tell Will first, and maybe even get some advice about how to calm his mother down.

He smiled as his wish came true and Will strode through the door. Will didn't take his eyes off Joe as he hung his hat on the open hook and sat down in the very chair Olivia had sat in mere hours earlier. He cocked his head to one side and leaned back, folding his arms over his chest.

Joe set down his poker and closed the door to the

forge, taking a seat at the desk in the corner of the shop.

"Well?" Will said finally, breaking the silence. Neither of the brothers was much of a talker, and someone had to do it.

"Well, what?" Joe folded his arms over his chest also, mimicking his brother's posture.

"Word travels fast around here, brother. Who's the lucky lady? Aunt Dorothy is saying she's an Indian, real dark.

"An Indian?" Joe said, his eyes widening. "No, she's not an Indian although I wouldn't mind if she was."

Will slapped his knee and stood, shaking his brother's hand. "Well, I'll be. Carol and I weren't sure we should believe it. She, of course, is excited to meet her sister-in-law and was hoping that Aunt Dorothy wasn't full of malarkey. Aunt Dorothy told Saffron and Saffron told us. They'll be happy to plan a wedding for you. You know how women are."

"Oh, so she went to make sure you knew before she went to Ma," Joe said slowly. "She happened to be there at the time, and threatened to go straight to Ma and stop it. Which is why I'm already married."

He looked up as Will straightened in his chair, his

THE BLACKSMITH'S MAIL ORDER BRIDE

eyes wide. "I beg your pardon? I heard you'd proposed, but..."

Joe ran his hands through his dark hair and poured two cups of coffee, setting one in front of his brother.

Will took a sip and spit it out. "This is stone cold. Maybe you've gone loco, brother."

Joe looked into the cup and then at the pot, which had been sitting on the counter since the day before, when Olivia had left. "Maybe I am. I'm not sure. But I'd decided I'd do anything rather than marry that horrible Jasmine Ma and Aunt Dorothy have picked out for me, and I'd already written an advertisement for a mail order bride. Olivia happened in yesterday and her whole place burned down and she doesn't have a nickel to her name. It seemed like the right thing to do when I saw her today."

"Olivia?"

"Yes, Olivia Blanchard. Do you remember the girl we met the other day?"

Will leaned forward, his elbows on his knees. "The one in the street having that ruckus with Jimmy Joe Walker? The one with the double-barreled shotgun?"

Joe quickly stood and began to pace, rubbing the

back of his neck. "Uh, I'd forgotten all about that. I just remembered how pretty she was when we saw her in the restaurant."

"That she is, brother. Very pretty. And seems smart, too. And—well, it's pretty clear she can handle herself with a shotgun."

Joe closed his eyes and hung his head as the realization washed over him that he hadn't thought this through much at all. Not only did he know very little about this girl, but what he *did* know was something that would be a thorn in his mother's side—beyond the fact of her mere existence as her new daughter-in-law—in that she used guns. And he was pretty confident that she used them well—and often. She would have to, being a rancher.

"It's done now, brother. Had the preacher do the ceremony right there in the mercantile before Aunt Dorothy could go to Ma. Thought it was best that way."

Will looked around the shop and peered out the window. "Where is she now?"

Joe sighed. "She was pretty much a sight after trying to put out the fire at her ranch all by herself all night. Sadie took her home to rest and get cleaned up. I'll be going over for supper—I guess to get to know her a little better before I take her home to Ma tomorrow."

Will whistled long and slow, then broke out in a deep laugh. "For somebody who hasn't done anything sudden in his entire life, this pretty much takes the cake, Joe."

Joe sat down at the desk and rested his chin in his hands. "I guess it sure does. And I'm not exactly sure how to go about this. Care to join me for tea this afternoon with Ma while I break the news? I could use the cavalry, I think."

Will studied his brother for a moment. "You know Ma and I are still on the outs because I married Carol. She's never forgiven me for marrying a girl who can't walk, even if she is the most wonderful person I've ever met."

"Yes, yes, I know. But I'm counting on strength in numbers. I think Ma mentioned last night Grandma will be there today for her weekly visit. That should make it a little easier, don't you think?"

Will laughed again. "I suppose I need to see her sometime. Pa's mother and Ma are like night and day. She might be able to talk some sense into her."

"It'd be the first time if she could. You ever seen that work? It doesn't surprise me that Grandma chose to move into her own house after Pa died. Those two are like oil and water."

"You're right about that. Can't promise that it'll help any, but I'd be willing to accompany you to witness your walk off the plank," Will said as he slapped his brother on the back and laughed.

CHAPTER 16

Four chimes sounded from the clock in the shop and Joe reluctantly set his tools down. Hammering molten steel seemed much more appealing than what he had to do now.

Part of it, anyway. He didn't look forward to seeing his mother and having to explain what had happened, but spending time with Olivia—his wife—had his stomach in a knot. The easy part was over. The actual wedding had been accomplished with little more fanfare than a daisy in Olivia's blackened hands, but now the hard part would begin. He'd have to get to know her, and they'd need to learn to live together amicably.

He lifted the heavy leather apron over his head and hung it in its place against the wall and set his tools where they belonged as he waited for his brother to come by. His dark brown hair smoothed back, he tugged on his coat and peered out the window, up and down Allen Street. With every tick of the clock, his stomach tightened more.

He looked up as the bells on the door jingled, into the smiling face of his brother.

"You ready for your execution?" Will said as he rubbed his hands together.

Joe reached into his pocket for the keys to the door. "Better to get it over with, I'd say," he grumbled as he closed the door and turned the lock.

"Carol thinks this is wonderful for you, Joe. I stopped in at the mercantile and got a little more information from Suzanne. We've been invited for supper as well. I hope that's all right with you." Will shoved his hands in his pockets and glanced sidelong at his brother. "Thought you could use some support there, too."

Joe hung his thumbs in the pocket of his vest as he eyed the house in front of them, its white picket fence gleaming in the afternoon sun. Vibrant flowers swayed in the breeze at the bottom of the porch. Joe couldn't exactly call it a happy home now, but it had been once. When he and Will were small and his father lived there with them.

As in times past, he smiled to see his grandmother on the porch, her gray hair in a neat bun. The sky had darkened a bit with an approaching monsoon, and she tugged her red, blue and gold shawl neatly around her as she stood and smiled at their approach.

"Grandma," Joe said warmly as he kissed her on the cheek when he'd reached the top of the porch stairs. Will did the same and she closed her eyes as she embraced them both tightly.

"You boys just keep getting more handsome every time I see you. Your father would be so proud," she said as she held Joe at arm's length and eyed him from head to toe.

Heat crept into his cheeks as he looked down at his boots. His grandmother—his father's mother—couldn't be more different than his mother. Where his mother was cold and distant, Grandma was warm and loving, something that kept both brothers visiting regularly to her little house on the outskirts of town. He had a fleeting thought that he should have—would have—talked to her about this big decision had there been time. She always gave good advice.

He turned to his mother as she stood, her knuckles white on the sides of the rocking chair. Her face was a similar shade and there was fire in her eyes as they flashed in his direction.

"Mother," he said. He leaned in to kiss her cheek and she turned away, her hand clutching a handkerchief tightly as she bit her knuckle.

He exchanged a glance with Will and realized that Will had yet to be acknowledged. He knew it had taken a lot for Will to accompany him, even though he hadn't said so, as their mother hadn't spoken to him since his wedding to Carol, and possibly never would.

"Don't mind her. She's having a little difficulty assimilating the news of your nuptials, a fact which I presume won't surprise you."

"Mother Stanton!" Joe's mother spat as she turned away, her back toward her family.

"Congratulations, Joe," his grandmother said as she looped her arm through his and guided him toward the tray of lemonade. "I believe this deserves a toast in honor of you and your new wife...oh, what is her name?"

"Olivia. Olivia Blanchard—er, Stanton," Joe said as he took the glass she held out toward him and Will did the same.

"Olivia. What a lovely name. And I hear she has had a mishap at her ranch. I do believe that the

Double Barrel Ranch is quite well known for their pork products, highly regarded. Why, I knew her grandfather, come to think of it. Fine man, he was," she said as she looked pointedly at their mother on the other side of the porch.

Joe's eyebrows rose as he sipped his lemonade. His grandmother knew more about his new wife than he did, and it appeared that his mother knew more than she wanted to know.

He cringed at the look of sadness in Will's eyes as he looked from his grandmother to his mother. "Thank you, Grandma. I hope you will like getting to know her."

"I should wonder the same about you, Joe," his mother said tersely, still not turning toward them.

His grandmother shook her head at her daughter-in-law. "I would think you'd want to have some relationship with your new daughters-in-law, Lucinda. Will and Joe are fine young men, and Carol is one of the kindest people I've met in my long life. I have no doubt that Joe knows exactly what he is doing, and that Olivia will be a fine addition to the family."

"Carol is quite fond of you, too, Grandma," Will said as he sat on the porch swing and smiled at the old woman. "Says you've got the heart of a lioness."

The older woman threw her head back and laughed, a rich, throaty sound. "I should say I've seen a thing or two in my lifetime, boy. And from what I've seen, kindness and family matter most."

"Kindness and family," Joe's mother said, almost in a whisper. "Kindness and family is what got your son killed, and took my husband and the boys' father away."

Joe's grandmother tightened her shawl around her shoulders, the beautiful golds and blues reminding him of having that very shawl wrapped around him in comfort many times after his father had died. It smelled of lavender like her, was part of her, and it comforted him even now. Especially as this didn't seem to be going very well.

"My dear, that is not the truth and you know it. Joe and Will are fine young men, and the women they choose also must be so. It couldn't be other."

"He doesn't even know this woman," the younger Mrs. Stanton said as she twisted her handkerchief in her hands. "I won't have it. It's bad enough that Will married that...that..."

Will stood from the swing, his eyes blazing. "Don't say it, Ma. Don't you dare. You have no right to judge her that way. You don't even know her."

His mother spun around, her eyes narrowed. "I

don't have to know her and I don't want to. She's not good enough for you. And now your brother's gone and done the same thing. I won't have it. This house is for upstanding, decent ladies who can take care of you both."

Will's fists clenched at his side and Joe stepped closer to him, his hand resting on his forearm.

"Will, she doesn't know what she's talking about. Carol is wonderful," he said as he glared at his mother.

"Lucinda," their grandmother said as she stepped forward to stand in between her daughter-in-law and grandsons. "That's mighty rich, coming from you. When was the last time you cooked a—well, cooked anything at all?"

Joe's mother paled even more, which he hadn't thought would be possible. At any other time, he might have laughed as his grandmother said what was completely true. She rarely lifted a finger in her own home, and to judge anyone else—it just wasn't right.

"I was hoping it wouldn't come to this, and that you'd see reason. Trust your boys, as they deserve to be trusted. They both love you, and they have a right to marry as they see fit."

"Mother Stanton, you know as well as I do that a

marriage should be a good match, a smart match, one for the right reasons. Joe doesn't even know this woman, and I won't have her in my house."

Sweat beaded down Joe's back as he watched the exchange he'd imagined *he* would be having with his mother played out between the two women. It seemed that his grandmother had made up her mind, and he was happy to have her on his side.

The elder Mrs. Stanton pursed her lips and set her chin. She pulled the shawl more tightly around her and sat in the rocking chair, moving slowly forward and back in the silence.

"Lucinda, don't do this," she said slowly, as she stood and turned toward her daughter-in-law. "It's not Joe's new wife who will not be welcome in this house, it is you."

CHAPTER 17

Olivia swished her finger in the water that was left in the bathtub as she shook her head. Sadie had brought her up to a bedroom on the second floor of her cozy home—Olivia carrying all of the water, though, after Sadie's twinge in her belly. As Sadie brought dresses from her room into the room, she'd gasped when she'd gotten a glimpse of herself in a proper mirror.

Not only was her face covered in remaining soot but there were lines running down her face where tears had run. Twigs hung from her hair from when she'd slept in the dirt, and her dress—once a light yellow—was still almost completely black.

She'd been in such a daze she hadn't noticed, and she couldn't imagine how Joe would have wanted to marry her in this state. It was almost funny, and she'd caught Sadie smiling at her a few times before she'd seen what she looked like. No wonder everyone was being so kind.

"You take a bath and get a good rest, Olivia. Tripp will be home shortly and he and I will make supper. Joe won't be here until around six or so, so you've plenty of time. You look like you could use even more sleep—among other things," she said as she poked her head through the open door.

Not long ago, Olivia had been unsure where or when she'd sleep next and she glanced around the room, taking in the blue lace curtains, amber lanterns on the nightstand and the beautiful quilt covering the inviting bed. She'd taken extra time brushing out the knots in her hair before she'd dipped her toe into the warm water. As she sunk in, holding her breath and settling under the warm water to wash her hair, her thoughts wandered to Joe, and her heart warmed. Even though she didn't know much about him, she trusted Suzanne and Sadie. Besides, any man who would marry her in such a state would have to be kind, wouldn't he?

After scrubbing off every inch of soot, she pulled on a night dress and settled down onto the soft bed for the second time, falling asleep almost as soon as her head hit the pillow—so soundly that no dreams haunted her.

Heavenly aromas from downstairs teased her awake several hours later. She stretched her sore, tender muscles and rose, dressing hurriedly so that she could help Sadie and Tripp—not like last time. She also looked forward to some company, any at all, to calm the nerves that had been tingling since she'd woken. It had taken a moment or two for her to remember that her house had burned down, she was penniless and had married a stranger and as the memories crashed through her, her nerves had awoken as well.

She'd chosen a deep green skirt and crisp white blouse from the wardrobe and dressed as quickly as she could. Sadie'd left a corset and stockings as well, along with newer, clean black shoes.

She took one last glance at herself in the mirror, reaching into her reticule to retrieve a tortoise shell comb that her mother had given her. She always kept it in her bag or it likely would have gone up in flames as well. Now, she swept her long, dark hair up behind her head, twisting it and fastening it with the comb and hoped her mother would approve of her decision. Braids, although practical, didn't seem suitable for her new husband.

The warm evening breeze carried voices through the open window and Olivia crossed over, pulling back the curtain and peeking out from the second story. Pink, purple and white clouds dotted the horizon to the west as the sun set behind the mountains, and from this second story, she thought maybe she could even see the ranch.

In the other direction, the thrum of Tombstone grew louder as the evening fell. Street lights were lit and their flames flickered with life as miners just getting off the day shift entered the restaurants, ice cream parlor and mercantile. Suzanne had sent word she'd be working late and would miss supper, but would stop by after she'd been able to close the mercantile.

"Hello, Olivia." Joe's deep voice caught her attention and she grinned, looking down toward the edge of Sadie's porch to see Joe smiling up at her tipping his hat.

She nodded and studied him more carefully. She hadn't seen him too many times—her wedding to him being one of the few—and she took a moment to admire his dark hair that reached his collar, his broad shoulders and rugged jaw. She'd certainly been fortunate that such a handsome, kind man had been willing to marry her in an instant and help her in her time of need.

Joe's brother stepped into view and waved up toward the window. "Hello, Olivia," he said as he turned back and lifted a lovely young woman out of his buggy, placing her in a chair he'd set out. The chair itself was lovely—padded, upholstered and with fringe trimming the frame—and the girl was even more beautiful.

"Carol, meet Olivia," Will said as he turned the chair toward the porch, nodding at Joe as they lifted it together and carried it up the steps. The young woman's eyes twinkled as she waved up at Olivia.

"Nice to meet you," Olivia said. "I'll be right down." Her cheeks flushed with excitement at the thought of spending the evening not only with her new husband, but her new family, and she was anxious to get to know Carol and Will as well.

She rushed down the stairs, stopping short as she reached the bottom. Will and Joe had brought Carol into the parlor, and Joe made proper introductions.

"Welcome to the Stanton family," Carol said as she shook Olivia's hand, her eyes twinkling.

Will didn't even try to stifle his laugh. "I'm not sure that's something that she's going to be grateful for," he said, clapping Joe on the back. "Especially after—"

"I, for one, am thrilled to have a new sister-in-law," Carol cut in as she nudged Will. "I'm certain we will get on famously, and everything else will resolve itself eventually."

Sadie rushed in from the kitchen, setting small plates of appetizers on the table in front of the settee. "Oh, Carol, could you excuse me for a moment? I really had wanted to help Sadie with preparations for the evening. She really shouldn't be doing all of this herself, especially at this time."

Olivia smiled at Carol as she nodded. Olivia barely knew Carol but thought she noticed a hint of sadness in her eyes as she watched Sadie return to the kitchen. She certainly would look forward to getting to know her new sister-in-law better later.

Olivia pushed through the swinging door to the kitchen and drew in a sharp breath. She rushed to Sadie's side and wound her arm over her friend's shoulder. "Are you all right?"

Sadie sat at the kitchen table, her forehead resting on her hands. She breathed in deeply, slowly, and eventually lifted her head. "I'm not sure. I—I think I'm fine, then I have these sudden sharp pains and I can barely stand."

Olivia glanced around the kitchen. "Where is Tripp? I thought he was going to help you with supper?"

Sadie smiled sheepishly as she said, "He couldn't get away from the restaurant quite yet, and I wanted you to rest."

"Sadie! We had this conversation earlier. You shouldn't be doing all of this on your own," Olivia said as she sat down beside Sadie at the table.

Sadie's eyes widened and she sat straight, her hand flying to her belly. "Oh, my," she said as she blinked rapidly.

"Sadie, I'm going to send for Tripp. And Suzanne. And the doctor. You just stay here for a moment," Olivia said as she rushed back into the parlor.

CHAPTER 18

Olivia closed the door behind her softly as she left Sage and Sadie alone. She stopped for a moment as Sadie groaned, Sage's muffled voice low and calm. Her experience on the ranch had taught her that birthing babies—well, pigs and the like—took its natural course and she imagined that it was the same with humans. But if that experience on the ranch told her anything, there was a long road between now and lying quietly with your newborn of any kind.

She took in a deep breath and squeezed the polished oak of the bannister at another sharp groan from Sadie. As she reached the bottom of the stairs and moved into the parlor, the low light of the lamps danced against the light yellow wallpaper in the cozy room as Tripp paced back and forth in front of the fire place.

"Everything will be fine," Olivia said in an attempt to calm the chef, who moments ago had been so confident in his kitchen at the restaurant.

Tripp ran his hand through his hair, his eyes filled with hope—and concern.

"It's too early, Olivia. Too early," he said as he leaned against the stone mantle and hung his head. A wedding portrait stood beside his hands, Sadie and Tripp happily in love. She picked it up and held it to the light of the fire.

In the photograph, Tripp sat on a chair with Sadie behind him, her hands on his broad shoulders. They'd met and married quickly, like she had, yet they both looked calm, sure—and in love at the time the photograph was taken. And now, they were having their firstborn.

She set the photograph back on the mantle, glancing at her new husband who sat on the velvet settee in the corner. He'd cut a handsome figure when he'd arrived with Carol and Will, but with all the commotion, she hadn't even had the opportunity to regard him much, and now, by the light of the fire she was able to look at him more closely.

He sat a bit awkwardly, leaning forward as if

ready to help if needed—at least that's how it seemed to her. She remembered the day she'd been at the mercantile and, although appearing a bit reluctant, her new husband and his brother had been poised at the ready to assist her in her altercation with Jimmy Joe Walker—just the memory of the horrid man twisted her stomach.

Had that been only days ago? It was hard for her to believe and after she placed a reassuring hand on Tripp's arm and shared a smile, she moved over toward her new husband and sat next to him—as close as she dared. She wanted to make this work, even through her discomfort, and was pleased when he smiled down at her.

She'd hoped to get to know him more at supper, but with the turn of events, that hadn't been possible.

A flash illuminated the room, followed by a sharp clap of thunder. The flames in the lanterns fluttered as they all turned toward the window. Streaks of lightning stretched across the sky as the wind picked up, a sure sign that rain was on the way.

"How far out did Sage say the doctor is?" Tripp asked as he wrung his hands, his knuckles white.

Joe crossed the room, resting his arm over Tripp's shoulders. "A ways out, but remember she also said it could be just early pains. Not the baby's time yet."

Sadie's unmistakable groan filtered down the stairs as all three turned toward the sound.

Olivia snuck a glance at Tripp as he said, "I know that this isn't the first baby in the world, and I shouldn't be so nervous."

"Sadie is in good hands, Tripp, and the cavalry is on its way," Olivia said as she parted the white, lace curtains. A covered buggy raced up the drive, a woman jumping from it almost before it had stopped.

"Tripp, what's going on? It's too early for the baby," Suzanne said as she crashed through the door, pulling off her bonnet and hanging it on the hook as Tripp took her coat. "Where is the doctor?"

"So glad you're here, Suzanne," Olivia said as she took her hand and pulled her up the stairs. "He'll be here shortly, we hope, but Sage is with her now."

"Thank you, Olivia. I'm so glad you were here." Suzanne rushed in the bedroom, wrapping her arms around Sadie as another groan escaped the future mother.

"It's not time yet," Sadie cried as Olivia closed the door once more. She resisted the urge to join them, imagining that too many people might be just the kind of help Sadie didn't need right now. She wrestled with feeling in the way and wanting to be of service. Suzanne's soft admonishments of comfort helped her decide, and she headed down the stairs, knowing Sadie was taken care of. Besides, the doctor should arrive at any moment.

As her boots touched the soft carpet at the bottom of the stairs, Joe entered the parlor from the kitchen, carrying a tray of biscuits and a pot of coffee. "I thought maybe since we missed supper, this might be helpful. Could be a long night," he said as he set the silver tray on the table by the settee. The thoughtful gesture touched Olivia, and she smiled up at her new husband as she poured a cup and handed it to Tripp. The cup chattered on the saucer as he took it from her.

"I'm sorry. I guess I'm still a little nervous," he said as he glanced up the stairs.

"Who wouldn't be, my man?" Joe asked as he looked out the window once again. "Where's that doctor?"

"He'd better get here soon," Sage said as she reached the bottom stair and crossed to the window herself. "Could be he's gotten stuck with the rain out at the Anderson place."

"Oh, I sure hope not," Tripp said as he leaned

over her shoulder and lightning streaked across the sky.

Olivia smiled as Joe came to stand behind her and his warm breath swept over Olivia's neck and she shivered. "I'm sure he'll be here shortly," she said as she reached for Joe's hand, surprised at how warm and dry it was under the circumstances.

"Joe, why don't we clean up in the kitchen," she said as she pulled him toward the door.

She wasn't sure what kinds of emergencies he'd met at the blacksmith shop, but he was definitely cool at the moment.

"Well, this certainly has been an interesting few days. Nothing I would have predicted," she said as she wrapped up what was to have been supper and placed it in the ice box. "At least they'll have plenty to eat if the baby comes."

Joe wiped his hands on a dishtowel as he finished up the rest of the dishes, placing them carefully on the counter. "I don't know where any of these go, but I imagine Suzanne does."

"Yes, she definitely does," Suzanne said as she pushed through the swinging door to the kitchen. "I can take care of that. Thank you for cleaning up. Sadie wanted to come down and do it." She shook her head and reached for a teacup. "Now I can assure her there's nothing for her to do but rest."

Olivia poured boiling water into a teapot and filled a plate with biscuits she'd seen while she was putting the food away. "Why don't I take this upstairs for you all? I would be in the room helping, but too many cooks..."

Suzanne laughed as she reached for the tray Olivia had set up. "What an appropriate comment, particularly in this house."

Joe cleared his throat and rubbed the back of his neck. "Suzanne, I know this wasn't the plan, but under the circumstances, maybe Olivia should come home tonight rather than tomorrow. I mean, to my home. Our home," he said, his hands behind his back as he shifted from foot to foot and leaned against the counter.

Olivia's stomach clenched. She'd had an inkling that she wasn't needed here—might even be in the way with more people coming—but it hadn't occurred to her that there was another choice. Even with the wedding, she'd not yet entertained the thought of moving into her husband's home. They'd not even had a private conversation yet.

Suzanne set the tray on the counter and crossed her arms over her chest. "Olivia, what say you? I know the plan was to have you stay here for a bit, and you are more than welcome. But she does have enough help here if you want to get on with your married life," she said as she smiled at both of them.

"I suppose—"

"Just a moment." Suzanne rested her hands on her hips and turned to Joe, squinting. "I feel a mite responsible for this union, and while I believe it is in the best interests of both of you, I have to ask, Joe. What about—well, what about your mother?"

Joe's eyebrows rose and he pushed himself away from the counter, squaring his shoulders. "I was hoping for a bit more time to ease her into this, but we have had a conversation. Aunt Dorothy made sure that everyone knew what had happened before I even had the chance."

"Ah, so she knows. How did she take it?" Suzanne asked as she sat down at the kitchen table, leaning forward on her elbows.

Joe glanced from Suzanne to Olivia and back to Suzanne, clearing his throat. "It wasn't quite as I'd hoped. But as I expected. Fortunately, my grandmother was there and she tried to talk some sense into her."

"Am I not wanted?" Olivia asked softly as she settled into the chair opposite Suzanne. She remembered the altercation with Joe's aunt, but surely they couldn't still be opposed to her arrival.

Suzanne reached for Olivia's hand, taking it in hers and squeezing. With a glance up at Joe, she said, "Joe's aunt and mother are unaccustomed to having people defy their wishes. It's not personal, Olivia. They just have set ideas as to how things should unfold. Joe's made his decision and I'm sure everything will be fine. Besides, we're always here if you need us," she said as she glanced at the door with another loud groan from Sadie.

Heat crept into Olivia's cheeks as she slowly turned to Joe. He looked as uncomfortable as she must, but even now she felt a sense of calm when in his presence. She had to make the leap at some point, and with the circumstances at Sadie's household, this felt like the right time—no matter what she'd be walking into. How bad could it be, anyway?

CHAPTER 19

The doctor hadn't yet arrived when Olivia and Joe drove away from the house. Sadie's groans had quieted and it seemed that the baby might not even come now.

She'd hugged Sadie goodbye and thanked her for her hospitality—and wished her good luck—before they'd gone, and Sadie had insisted she take the clothes she'd filled the wardrobe with. Olivia had tried to argue, but Sadie wouldn't take no for an answer, the picture of kindness even in this state.

Lightning flashed in the distance and the scent of rain carried on the wind, but so far it was dry where they were. It was a short drive from Sadie's house to Joe's, she was told, and she'd asked if he'd stop by the livery so she could retrieve what few remaining belongings she'd managed to hoist into the small buggy.

"I know this is all quite sudden," Joe said as he helped her down from the buggy and unlocked the livery.

She breathed a sigh of relief as she stroked the noses of her horses, pleased to see that they were safe and sound in the livery. Out of the corner of her eye, she spotted a basket of apples, happy that they were treated kindly.

The earthy aroma of hay and manure reminded her of the ranch—her barn, specifically—and was oddly comforting when her life had changed so suddenly, as Joe had just pointed out.

"If someone had told me mere days ago that we'd be doing this now, I doubt I would have believed them," she said as she reached around to the back of the buggy, pulling aside the blanket she'd used to cover what of her possessions she could carry.

"Nor would I," Joe said as he reached into the basket for an apple, holding it out to one of Olivia's horses.

He leaned back against the wall of the livery and pushed his black hat up on his forehead. His eyes met Olivia's and he crossed his arms over his chest.

He shifted his weight from one boot to the other and waited a moment before he spoke.

"Olivia, I think there are a couple of things we should talk about."

Her hand stopped midway into the back of the buggy as her stomach clenched. There had been no time to even think of the things they should talk about, but they were married now and she supposed it had to happen.

"Yes?" she said as she pulled aside her skirts and sat on a barrel next to her horses. She almost smiled at the expression on his face that was clearly discomfort, bordering on horror.

"I hope this isn't awkward, but I wanted you to know that I've prepared a bedroom for you—your own. Even though we're married, I want you to know that I don't expect—well, I don't expect relations until—or if—that's something that you want, too," he said, the words tumbling out of his mouth in fits and spurts.

Relations? How had she not thought about that? Even standing there in the mercantile, covered in soot with a lone daisy in her hand, it hadn't crossed her mind. Since it hadn't, she was grateful that he had brought it up, and his offer was considerate. He had every right to expect otherwise, but this had come upon him as quickly as it had her, and maybe it was best if they ease into the rest. Besides, his mother may not want this and she'd seen many a formidable adversary in mothers who didn't like their daughters-in-law.

And hadn't Joe mentioned earlier that she'd refused to speak with Will and his wife since they'd been married? What kind of woman could turn her back on someone as warm and wonderful as Carol? And her own son, who seemed to be a stand-up young man. Just like his brother.

Olivia had very little experience dealing with people. Things were cut and dry, black and white at the ranch. Something needed to happen and you did it. She'd never had to deal with anyone who couldn't see what was right in front of them.

"Thank you," was all she knew to say. "I—I appreciate that. Things have happened very quickly."

"They have. Mother isn't expecting us tonight and may be abed even now. In fact, that would be wonderful," he said as he pushed himself from against the wall and crossed over to the buggy.

She stood on her tiptoes to reach into the back and gripped her steel bucket of tools, ones that had been her father's. She'd found his hammer and his hatchet, throwing them in the bucket as she'd raced around the fire. She handed it to Joe, his eyebrows rising as their hands brushed when he gripped the bucket, his warmth settling her nerves.

"What are these?"

She looked up into his smiling eyes, the brown deep and kind. Her eyes fell to her boots as she shuffled her feet. "I had so little time to gather anything with the fire raging. Those are a few of my father's prized possessions. Ones that he valued most," she said as she looked up again. She thought he might be laughing at her, but he lowered his eyes and nodded.

"I have some similar things of my father's. He passed away rather suddenly when I was very young. They are simple things, but all I have left," he said as she turned back toward the wagon.

"Oh, my," she said, remembering Suzanne had mentioned he'd lost his father as well. "So your mother is a widow, then."

"She is, and I believe that's why—well, that was when things changed," he said softly as he set the bucket in the corner of the livery.

She reached into the back and closed her eyes as her fingers wrapped around her father's *most* prized possession, the cold steel familiar and comforting. She pulled it out and gripped the heavy weight with both hands, smiling as she turned toward Joe, anxious to show him.

She stiffened abruptly as she looked up at him, her smile melting from her face in an instant.

He faced her, his palms outward as he took a slow step backward, his eyes riveted on her. His face had blanched and she frowned, confused, as she looked from him to the shotgun in her hands.

"This is my pa's," she said slowly as she held it out to him. He took two more slow steps backward, stopping only when he had bumped against the wall. "Joe, what is it?" she said as she took a step forward, close enough now to see the sweat beading on his forehead.

"I—so that's your pa's?" he said as he raked his sleeve over his forehead and pulled his hat down further, shading his eyes.

"Yes. He'd had it since before I was born. I learned to shoot with it," she said as she cocked her head and rested the barrel of the shotgun on the hay-covered dirt floor. Surely he'd handled guns before. He was a blacksmith, after all, even if he was a city-dweller. "Are you all right?"

"Yes, yes, I'm fine." He tugged at his shirt collar and averted his eyes, reaching into the barrel for another apple. "Why don't you put that over in the corner? Don't think we'll need it at the house."

She hefted the weight of the gun to her hip. Could she leave it? She hadn't slept without it a single night since Pa died. She'd left it in the livery tonight since Sadie was having her baby. It seemed important to him, though, so she wrapped it in a blanket and placed it in the corner, settling it carefully.

She turned toward Joe. There was so much to learn—everything, really. She didn't even know this man she now called her husband.

She had very little to call her own, everything else on the dirt back at the ranch, and she quickly retrieved the remainder of her belongings. As she turned toward the door, Olivia paused for a moment, watching his deliberate movements. She hadn't meant to alarm him—clearly they came from very different situations. She wanted to know more about him and tell him more about herself. She imagined they'd have the opportunity, but for now she needed to meet his mother—and see what she'd gotten herself into.

CHAPTER 20

The ride from the blacksmith shop to his house was short—he frequently walked to work—but it was enough time for his heartbeat to slow. Between telling his new wife that he expected no marital relations from her and staring down the barrel of a shotgun, the last hour had beaten even Sadie's baby groans for nerve-racking.

They'd fallen silent on the ride and the thunder had ceased. The creaking of the buggy wheels was the only thing disturbing the peace of the night. He'd lit the lantern on the side of the buggy, although he could have made it home with the light of the moon now that the clouds had cleared. Better safe than sorry, he always said, so he'd done it anyway.

It could have been that he just didn't want to rush

home. He'd thought he had at least one more night to work on Ma. Even with his grandmother's help—and cryptic threat—he had a sneaking suspicion that this may not be easy. If his mother hadn't spoken to Will and Carol for these past months, it didn't bode well for her accepting a complete stranger into her home so suddenly.

But what his grandmother had said confused him. He hadn't had time to really think that one through. He'd been prepared, as a result of his decision, to move elsewhere but to hear his grandmother say that it would be his mother who would be unwelcome shook the ground under his feet. He and Will hadn't even talked about it as they'd hurried to Sadie and Tripp's, but what did that mean?

As a result of the conversation that he'd hurried out of between his grandmother and his mother—he hadn't wanted to be late to meet with his new bride—he was unsure what he'd be walking into. As he approached the house, he snuck a glance out of the corner of his eye at Olivia and hoped that if it couldn't be peaceful, at least it might be civil.

He wished he didn't even need to be thinking about that. He'd been around her a fair amount, now, and the scent of vanilla floating on the breeze toward him was anything but unpleasant. When he'd seen her in the light of the lamps at Sadie's house, she was almost unrecognizable. The time he'd spent laughing and talking with her before the tide turned before supper was most pleasant, and he was struck by her good nature, even after everything that had happened to her. He wanted to ask more about what had happened at the ranch, how it might have happened, but he'd wanted to hear her laugh more and thought it a conversation best left to another time.

Maybe in a few days she might want to go back to the ranch. He'd love to see it, see where she'd grown up, what she did—what was left of it, anyway—but was unsure she'd want to. Besides, it might be good for her to take some time to get to know his mother while he was at work. At least he hoped it might be.

As he studied her, she pointed to a house as they approached. The lights burned low in the parlor, and he hoped that meant his mother had retired for the evening. He didn't see his grandmother's buggy as he craned his neck and was sorry that she hadn't stayed. He was hoping for reinforcements.

"Is that your house?" she said, finger raised at the white clapboard directly in front of them. His mother had taken great care in planting flowers at the base of the porch stairs, a great victory in the midst of the desert. They swayed in the warm evening breeze, their bright reds and yellows in stark contrast to the white of the house, vibrant even in the moonlight.

He slowed the buggy as they pulled up and looked at the house, seeing it as Olivia might. What did her house look like? Or what had it looked like, as the case was.

"It's charming." Olivia's eyes darted around the house, from the flowers to the second story, a smile creeping across her face.

The tension in his shoulders eased a bit as they reached the house—Olivia was still smiling. She must not have noticed the curtains in the upstairs bedroom part and fall back together several times—his mother's bedroom. At least that was one question answered for him. She was in her room and likely intended to remain there. He'd never really thought she wouldn't, but it was good to know what he'd be walking into. What they'd be walking into.

But as his mother was upstairs with only one small lamp burning in the parlor, he'd be able to address that tomorrow. He'd never had the opportunity to tell his mother that Olivia wouldn't be coming home with him this evening, so she'd made

THE BLACKSMITH'S MAIL ORDER BRIDE

the decision to retire early thinking they'd be arriving together.

He silently was grateful for the reprieve—tomorrow would be soon enough. And even though Olivia had rested earlier in the day, he'd noticed her yawning on the drive and he would be happy to end the evening himself.

"I'll get you settled in your room before I put the horses away for the night," he said as he tied them to the hitching post at the bottom of the stairs.

"Thank you." She reached for the hand he'd extended toward her, and as she took the last step down, his arm found its way around her waist. She stopped and looked up at him, the moonlight glinting from her eyes.

How had it happened that he was taking this lovely creature into his home as his wife? She may have had some difficulties, but she seemed genuinely kind—and fearless—and he was fascinated by her.

He realized he hadn't let go of her hand and the smoothness of it surprised him. His own were rough with callouses, born from many hours hammering steel. He would have thought hers would be the same from work on the ranch, and he certainly wouldn't have minded, but they weren't.

The thought of Sadie and her coming newborn

crossed his mind. Would this be what he would have with Olivia? Emotion he hadn't felt in many years swept over him and he impulsively tipped his hat at this beautiful young woman—his wife—and lifted her warm hand to his lips, brushing them slowly across her skin.

His eyes closed as her scent washed over him once more, and her other warm hand rested gently on his cheek. Pleased he hadn't startled or insulted her, he straightened, his heart light as he was met with a sparkling smile.

"You certainly are jovial for having been through so much these past few days," he said as he removed his hat and offered her his arm.

She looped hers through his and smiled up at him, her green eyes framed by long, dark eyelashes. She looked down for a moment before meeting his eyes once again.

"I've never been much of a gambler, Joe, but I always have tried to make lemonade from lemons."

"Lemons, am I?" he said as he squeezed her hand, his smile wide.

Startled, she looked up at him. "Oh, no, I meant..."

He nodded at her once again. "I'm teasing. In truth, we've both been presented with buckets of lemons. But I'm beginning to feel that together, we may just make the tastiest lemonade this side of the Mississippi."

He calmed at her lovely laugh, surprised that it felt familiar and calming to him. She stood on her toes and pecked him on the cheek, his hand flying to where her lips brushed his tingling skin.

"Thank you," he said as he gestured toward the front door.

"No, thank you." She offered him a slight curtsey before she looped her arm in his again.

"Shall we go inside, Mrs. Stanton? Would you like to see your new home?"

Olivia lifted her skirts with her free hand and nodded. "I'd like that very much, Mr. Stanton," she said as they started up the steps.

As they reached the top of the porch steps, it was clear that the parlor was empty and Joe felt a swoosh of relief wash over him at the confirmation. He took one last glance up to his mother's room, though, stiffening as he saw the curtains fall back together.

It didn't matter what she thought, he reminded himself. The evening had been lovely and he looked forward to getting to know his bride more tomorrow. If he was lucky, his mother would just stay out of their way.

CHAPTER 21

The sun glowed below the horizon, not yet cresting the top of the mountains. It wasn't sunrise proper yet, but Olivia had gotten up before the sun for so many years that she panicked, her first thought that the chickens would be so hungry they'd peck her as she spread the chicken feed.

She sat up in bed and looked around, her surroundings foreign to her. She listened for the chickens and was met with silence. It took a moment for her to realize that what chickens she'd strained to hear were in the distance...not hers, and not here.

She stretched, her muscles still objecting to moving as much as they had in the past few days. Rubbing the back of her neck, she walked toward the washbasin, delicate flowers painted on the porcelain. She poured cool water from the matching pitcher and splashed her face, taking in a deep breath and blinking her eyes as she looked about the room she'd awoken in.

Joe had kindly brought her very few things up to the room the evening before, and she'd secretly been relieved that his mother was nowhere to be found. No light peeked from under the door to the room Joe indicated was hers, and although it might have been better to just take the bull by the horns last night, she felt more rested today and ready to meet her fate.

The bed had been comfortable—more comfortable than her own—and she'd fallen into a dreamless sleep after wrapping herself up in the cozy comforter, also adorned with flowers. She'd never seen so many flowers, from the rug to the washbasin, the curtains and even the towel she now set back down on the vanity.

She dressed quietly and quickly, choosing a dress that Sadie had given her that was more appropriate for work—a day dress. She didn't know what was in store for the day, but it must involve work. What else would she do?

She fingered the dress she'd arrived in, soot

sticking to her skin. She found an older piece of cloth folded in the wardrobe—no flowers—and wrapped the dress in it. Once she knew where the washtub was, maybe she could salvage it. It had been one of her mother's and although it was singed several places on the sleeve and the hemline, it would be worth the trouble.

Her eyes closed, she remembered the last time she had seen her mother—in this very dress—and wished she were here now. She'd had very little female companionship since then, only seeing her friends in town on the odd occasion she drove in, and the memory of her mother was soft and sweet.

"Olivia? Are you awake?" followed a soft rap on her door. Joe—he was up early, too.

She crossed to the door, flinging it open, to the sight of a fresh bouquet of flowers, the same as the ones she'd seen in front of the house the evening before. He smiled as he thrust them in her direction.

"Good morning. I trust you slept well," he said as he took a step back from the door.

"I did." Olivia reached for the flowers, bending her head toward them as she inhaled deeply. The scent of roses captured her, their beautiful orange and pink fairly vibrating in her hand.

"Roses. However do you grow these here in the

desert?" Her eyes grew wide at the explosion of color in her hand.

Joe looked down the hallway toward his mother's room. He lowered his voice and said, "My mother tends them. Spends most of her time in the garden, and I must say we all are rewarded for her efforts."

"Quite a talent she has," Olivia said as she searched her room for a vase. She found one on her nightstand and filled it with water, arranging the flowers loosely. "I tried for years and finally gave up out on the ranch. My time was better spent on things like onions and tomatoes, and even that was a challenge."

"We get our vegetables at the mercantile here. I suppose living in town will be a big change for you," Joe said as he gestured for her to follow him downstairs.

"I should say so. I rarely went farther than the cellar after we'd canned for the year. Except for ham and bacon...had to go all the way to the smokehouse for that."

"We get that at the mercantile, too. The best ham and bacon you've ever tasted."

Her skin prickled at the mention of the ham and bacon at the mercantile. She couldn't blame Joe—how would he know that those products had come from her farm for years, the very ones he thought were the best? But now…there was no way to guess where Suzanne and Sadie would receive their meat.

"Have you heard anything about Sadie? The baby?" Olivia followed him down the stairs as the sun peeked over the top of the mountains to the east. "She could have had a baby by now."

Joe ushered her into the kitchen and she sat down at the table to a steaming mug of tea and a plate of lovely pastries. She looked around for Joe's mother, and in her absence, her eyebrows rose. Joe must have done this for her. She'd always been up early to make breakfast for her father and Percy—and then just Percy. She hadn't been served breakfast since her mother died.

"I hope you like pastry," he said as he sat down opposite her at the kitchen table.

"It's lovey, Joe. I—it's lovely." She dumped two teaspoons of sugar into her tea and a dollop of cream.

She'd been given a quick tour of the house the previous evening. Now, in the light of day she could see more. Flowers, everywhere. Porcelain tea service painted with flowers stood in the corner, and the curtains that swayed in the breeze—flowers. Even the flatware had flowers engraved on the handles.

Joe turned toward the parlor as the grandfather clock chimed. "Olivia, I sorely wanted to introduce you to my mother, but I'd scheduled early appointments at the shop hoping to leave early to bring you home. That—well, you know how that turned out."

Olivia's stomach tightened at the thought of meeting Joe's mother on her own. Nothing that she'd heard about her had been promising, or even very good. But she lived on a ranch. She'd handled rattlesnakes, for goodness sake. How bad could it be?

She took another look around the room, especially at the flowers. Someone who enjoyed and cultivated such beauty couldn't be all bad. She squared her shoulders and turned back to Joe.

"Please, go ahead. I appreciate your concern, but I'm sure we'll be just fine."

Joe frowned, but stood. "All right. If you're sure. I'll send word about Sadie as soon as I can find out. I am just over at the shop if you need anything."

He glanced over his shoulder at her once more as he put on his hat and headed down the porch steps. She waved and smiled bravely, closing the door only after he'd rounded the bend.

She rested her forehead on the back of the door, taking in a deep breath. She pushed herself up and turned, and stared straight into the eyes of a woman standing at the bottom of the stairs.

Her breath hitched in her throat as the woman said, "Who are you, and what are you doing in my house?"

CHAPTER 22

"I'll stay out of your way if you'll stay out of mine," Mrs. Stanton finally said after she stared at Olivia for what seemed like an eternity. She'd introduced herself—Mrs. Stanton didn't seem all that surprised, and Olivia knew that she'd been aware of her impending arrival, just not the timing—but she had just played along and explained.

The woman had stood stock still at the bottom of the stairs the entire time, her dark locks flecked with gray drawn back into a severe bun at the nape of her neck. Olivia thought she'd seen her once at the mercantile—she couldn't say when—and she'd appeared just as severe then.

Now, she was dressed in black, a brooch tight at her neck. There wasn't a hint of another color anywhere on her—she stood in stark contrast to the colorful flower patterns surrounding even the parlor.

She hadn't gone into great detail about what had happened at the ranch. Her new mother-in-law hadn't even feigned interest. When she'd finished, she'd made her proclamation and turned toward the kitchen, leaving Olivia alone in the foyer.

She awkwardly shifted from foot to foot. The woman clearly didn't want her there. Honestly, she was, after all, an intruder in the woman's home, for all intents and purposes. She glanced out the window in the direction of the blacksmith shop. Should she fetch Joe? Would that make this any easier?

No, she couldn't bother him at work. She smoothed her skirts, grateful at least that she wasn't standing in her dress covered in soot, and steeled her resolve.

"Mrs. Stanton, I realize that this is sudden, my arrival. It's sudden for Joe and me, too," she said as Mrs. Stanton poured herself a cup of tea from the pot Joe had left ready. She reached for a pastry on the plate, taking a bite and chewing slowly as she stared at Olivia.

Olivia waited for her to speak and she started to

squirm. This wasn't going the way she'd thought it would. A general, introductory conversation would have been better than this...this silence.

"Your flowers are beautiful, Mrs. Stanton. Your garden is quite impressive. I was never able to grow flowers at the ranch. Only hogs. And some vegetables. And you have so many types. It must be a challenge to keep it free of varmints. Especially rabbits. They are cute, some people think, but they can ruin a garden overnight if you aren't vigilant. And..."

Mrs. Stanton blinked blandly at Olivia as she finished her tea and Olivia rambled. Olivia could kick herself. What was she even talking about? Rabbits? And vegetables?

"Young lady, by your own admission you've no business in a flower garden."

Heat crept up her neck as her voice trailed off and silence fell heavily again. She tugged at her sleeve as she looked down at her shoes.

Mrs. Stanton placed her cup and saucer in the sink and turned toward Olivia.

"I have a suggestion. You stay out of my garden and mind yourself. I'm sure Joe will show you where things are around here. The wash basin, things of that ilk," she said as she brushed a speck of dust off of her sleeves. "I'm sure you're more suited to that kind of thing."

She knew she *was* good at those kinds of things, but somehow it didn't feel like a compliment coming from this woman.

The woman brushed past her and pushed the swinging door to the parlor. The scent of starch swept past and Olivia crinkled her nose. She glanced at the woman's black dress and noticed it was stiff as a board. She imagined there'd be a lot of starching to do in this household, something she'd never bothered with before.

Mrs. Stanton turned back just before she crossed the threshold, one of her eyebrows raised and a corner of her mouth turning up. "Oh, and I don't cook. It's all yours," she said as she nodded curtly and let the door swing closed.

CHAPTER 23

Small spice jars clattered as Olivia placed them in neat rows in the cupboards. She'd spent the morning doing a complete inventory of the kitchen. If it was to be her purview, she was going to do a solid job of it. She certainly wasn't going to give this sour woman anything additional to complain about.

She'd already started on supper and at the same time had prepared something for Joe for lunch. Nothing fancy—there was rarely an opportunity to make anything fancy at the ranch. Supper would be ham and potatoes with carrots. She'd found the ham in the cellar and her mood lifted when she realized it was from the Double Barrel Ranch. It was a credit to their skill that the ham was still good and had been stored in the cool root cellar for quite a while.

She stirred the potatoes that had been simmering on the stove and leaned over, inhaling spices that comforted her to her bones. This would be her first supper in her new home and she wanted it to be perfect. What great good fortune that she had one of her own hams to impress her new family with.

Slowly parting the floral curtains, she peeked out into the garden on the north side of the house. The rolling hills beyond the cactus were green from the monsoons—they'd gotten plenty of rain lately, almost too much—and she spied movement from the corner of her eye.

Mrs. Stanton, covered in a wide-brimmed hat and leather gloves, sat on an overturned bucket, pulling weeds from amongst her flowers. Piles of weeds dotted the perimeter of the wrap-around porch. She'd clearly been at it for hours, likely most of the time Olivia had been in the kitchen—her kitchen now.

The small, separate patch away from the house was rimmed with chicken wire and Mrs. Stanton reached over gingerly. She'd thought she'd been rambling, but maybe what she'd said had been accurate. They must have varmints here, too, or wouldn't need fencing.

Olivia backed away from the window as Mrs. Stanton took off her hat and wiped sweat from her brow with a floral handkerchief. Saying hello didn't seem appropriate—she'd made her desires clear that they keep a wide berth from one another.

Maybe there was some way she could—

She let the curtains fall as Joe approached the house, whistling happily. A package wrapped in brown paper and twine was tucked beneath his arm and he fairly jumped up the porch steps.

Olivia's heart quickened as his whistle continued into the parlor, where he shrugged off his coat and jauntily threw his hat onto the peg by the door.

He strode through the swinging door just as Olivia set plates of meat and cheese on the table, along with a pitcher of iced tea.

"And she can cook!" Joe rubbed his hands together. "Can life get any better?"

Olivia's heart soared as she reached for his shoulders, turning him toward the sink and handing him a kitchen towel. "Well, she thinks she can cook. Guess the proof will be in the pudding."

"Pudding, too?" Joe's eyebrows rose and his eyes twinkled.

"No, but maybe some for dinner if I have all I need," she said as she sat down at the table.

Joe loaded his plate and licked his finger quickly before wiping it on the napkin he'd set in his lap. "Mmm, this is delicious," he said as he leaned back in his chair.

Olivia smiled and parted the curtains, pointing at his mother. "Should I call her in for lunch?" she asked, turning back to Joe.

"How has it gone with you two today?" he asked, leaning forward as he peered out the window.

"I wouldn't say particularly well. We had a very brief exchange, where she told me to stay out of the garden and I could have the kitchen." She brushed away a dark curl that had escaped from her bun, quickly pinning it back in place.

"Oh, I see," he said, leaning forward on the table as he pushed his empty plate forward. "I imagine that would be her optimal division of labor. She doesn't cook."

Olivia's hand rose to her cheek as she, too, bent forward and looked out the window. "At all?" she asked, incredulous. How could a woman—a woman with a family—not cook?

"Not since Pa died. He loved suppertime, loved

her, and when he passed—well, she didn't care much for food or for cooking."

Joe had turned from the window and cast his eyes down on the floral plate before him.

"These dishes—everything here, really—are beautiful. She must have taken great pride in taking care of her family."

"Yes, she did. Once." He cleared his throat and glanced up at Olivia, meeting her eyes.

His dark eyes clouded, and she asked softly, "How old were you when your father passed?"

He blinked a few times quickly and ran his hand through his hair. "I was sixteen and Will was fourteen. Quite a few years ago, but..."

He broke their gaze and looked back out the window toward his mother.

She waited for a moment, then said, "No matter how much time has passed, the memory seems to stay fresh."

"For some of us more than others," he said abruptly as he pushed himself back from the table and gathered the dishes from the table.

"I'll do that," Olivia said quickly as she reached for the plate in his hand. He had a shop to run, after all, and if her only job was to cook—well, then she'd do it all. After the ranch, it hardly felt like enough to keep a woman busy for an entire day, after all.

"I'm making ham and potatoes for supper, if that's all right with you and your mother," she said as she stirred the potatoes on the stove. "I made myself at home in the kitchen after your mother—well, I hope that's all right."

"Of course it's all right. I'm just pleased that there haven't been fireworks. I suppose that's as good as it's going to get right now." He moved closer to her and took her hand. "I'm sorry, Olivia. You deserve better than the silent treatment."

Her hand tingled at his touch and she nodded in thanks. "Maybe I can dazzle her with my cooking. I could do much better if I had things from my own kitchen."

"Do you think that anything might be salvageable?" Joe asked, leaning against the counter and folding his arms over his chest.

Olivia tapped her finger against her cheek. "I'm not exactly sure. I did gather everything as fast as I could, but the whole night is a blur in my memory."

"Since she's not speaking to you, I suppose it wouldn't matter if we took a trip out to the ranch tomorrow to see. If we leave at sunrise, we could be back before dark. If that's something that would interest you," he said as he cocked his head and their eyes met.

She hadn't really considered going back so soon. She peered out the window at Mrs. Stanton's back and realized that their relationship certainly wasn't going to change over night. And he was right. They weren't speaking to each other, so what harm could there be in taking a look at the ranch?

"I'll get some food ready for us. I know there's nothing left as the kitchen was the first to go up in flames," she said as she pulled her hand away from Joe's warm one.

He was kind to offer. She should certainly be grateful and steel herself against what she might find. She'd never found nor heard about Percy, and she certainly didn't want to face that adventure alone.

CHAPTER 24

Olivia grabbed the side of the buckboard as it lurched through the stream bed. The few inches of water in the wash from the last monsoon ambled past the palo verde trees and high reeds. She peered out from under her blue bonnet at the sky—not a cloud in sight, something she and Joe had both commented on when they'd set out from his house at sunrise.

The time since had been fairly quiet, interspersed with commentary about the terrain, the road, the people who lived on the ranches that dotted the road. Once they'd passed the town of Whetstone—which was really just a small grouping of houses west of Tombstone—she'd fallen silent again as her nerves got the best of her. So much had changed in her life in an incredibly short period of time. The ranch she'd called home was gone—or most of it, anyway—Percy was nowhere to be found and she was not only homeless but penniless.

She glanced over at Joe, his strong jaw set as he followed her directions, leading the horses with ease over the sometimes rough terrain. He stiffened, his eyes trained on a rise beyond the next outcropping. After their dip into the San Pedro Valley, where the river ran, they'd climbed steadily into low-lying hills that eventually turned into the majestic mountains that surrounded the valley.

She followed his line of sight and caught some movement—riders, who turned their horses back down the ridge and disappeared.

Joe's grip on the reins had tightened and he squinted in the direction of the disappearing riders.

"Looked like Indians," he said slowly, his eyes not leaving the ridge. "Are they a problem for you out here?"

"We had some trouble a few years ago, a couple of different tribes angling for land out here. But lately, no. They've been peaceful—even trading with a few of us."

"Trading?"

Olivia held her hand over her bonnet, searching

the horizon. "Yes. Believe it or not, they like ham and bacon, and they have some very interesting things to trade."

"They do, do they?" Joe said. "I've not worked with them much in the shop. In the beginning, they came in and asked us to fix their guns but—well, since we don't work on guns, they took their business elsewhere."

Joe's unease when she'd lifted her shotgun from her buggy had perplexed her. She didn't know him all that well, and from the pained expression on his face she wasn't sure she should ask.

"Why is it that you don't?"

Joe took a sidelong glance at her from the corner of his eye. He looked up at the ridge once more, hesitating before he answered.

"Guess you might as well know as you're my wife now."

She waited a bit longer, her mind racing with things that could have caused his aversion. Where she had grown up, they were a necessity. You never knew when a coyote might venture too close to the smokehouse.

Joe squirmed on the seat of the buckboard. "When pa died, we were pretty young, as I told you. But we'd apprenticed in the shop for many years and knew what we were doing. Will, in fact, is a genius when it comes to fixing things."

Olivia had liked Will when she'd met him—easygoing and his wife had been charming. Not at all bitter that she was confined to a chair with wheels. She imagined that he and Joe worked well together.

"You seem to have made a great success of it," she said as she rested her hand on his forearm, hoping to encourage him to continue.

"We have. But we wouldn't have gotten the chance if my grandmother hadn't stepped in," he said as he pulled his hat further down his forehead. "Ma wanted to sell it, but Grandma said we needed a future. With what happened to Pa, Ma—well, she really suffered. Didn't speak for months."

"As now," Olivia said under her breath, not wanting him to stop.

Joe rested his elbows on his knees as he leaned forward, encouraging the horses through the gates Olivia pointed toward, the entrance to the Double Barrel Ranch.

"Yes. When things aren't going well for her, she gets very quiet. But I suppose we've grown accustomed to it. I hadn't noticed much until Will left. She talks quite a bit when she has a mind to—just not about anything of substance."

"What made her change her mind?" Olivia asked after a bit, gazing up at the cottonwood trees that lined the drive to what used to be her home.

Joe glanced quickly at her before craning his neck to peer around the small hill that the road curved around. He cleared his throat and straightened in his seat.

"We had to agree not to work on guns. Of any kind."

Olivia was startled away from gazing at the trees and turned to look at Joe.

"What? Why? There are so many guns here on the frontier, it would be a good sight of business to lose, I would imagine."

Joe nodded slowly. "It was. But with how things turned out with Pa, Ma was adamant. Sell the shop or agree."

Olivia's grip tightened on his arm as they rounded the bend. She sucked in a sharp breath as she spied the remains of her ranch. Blackened wooden boards fell askew around what had been the smokehouse and the fence surrounding it lay in heaps of ash around the perimeter.

She tore her gaze from the smokehouse to the barn next to it—or what was left of the barn that Percy had lived in. She'd had her two horses with her when she'd arrived, and the other two working horses were nowhere to be found at the time. Soft whinnies sounded from the small grove to the right of the ranch and her heart calmed as she turned, smiling as the two horses drank from the water trough she'd filled before she left in case they returned. At least she wouldn't be looking for their bodies here shortly. Only Percy's.

"My goodness. You tackled this all alone?" Joe asked. He whistled and sat up straight in the buckboard, pushing his black hat back up his forehead.

Olivia followed his gaze to the main house—or what was left of it. Her heart sank as she raked her eyes over what had been her home. Most of it lay in rubble, only part of the barn standing on the far west of the structure. Not even the porch steps remained, and she had a vague recollection of the sound they'd made as she'd fallen back, exhausted, on the dirt as she gave up trying to save anything more.

Joe pulled up slowly, tightening the reins and bringing the horses to a stop beyond the cactus that also lined the drive, under the big oak tree that had stood proudly as a sentinel in front of their house. The swing her pa had made for her when she was a girl swayed softly in the light breeze.

The brake of the buckboard squeaked as Joe

pushed it down with his foot and stepped out, coming around to help Olivia out, but she had both feet on the ground before he arrived and walked slowly toward the house.

"Now, Olivia, be careful. It's not likely very steady in there," he said as she put one foot in front of the other, feeling as if she were in a dream.

As she reached the bottom of what had been the stairs, she turned, tears pricking her eyes. "Joe. Joe, I..."

He'd followed her closely and as she turned, the scent of him replaced the familiar smell of soot that had already invaded her nostrils. She looked up at him just as her tears escaped, cascading down her cheeks. His deep, brown eyes reflected her pain, and as he reached out to her, she crumpled in his arms, not sure if she could look again at the wreckage that was her life.

He held her as sobs racked her body, and she clung to him as if there was nothing else in the world—and there wasn't. She'd thrown in her lot with him, for better or for worse, and now that the "worse" was right before her very eyes once more, she melted into his strong arms.

CHAPTER 25

Joe stroked Olivia's hair and he held her as tightly as he dared. Her body shook with her sobs and he brushed her waves of brown hair back that had escaped when she'd pulled off her bonnet and thrown it on the ground. He rested his chin on the top of her head as he took in the sight—what a night that must have been. What looked like a smokehouse and part of a barn dotted the landscape, some remaining blackened boards still smoldering.

As she shook with tears, his brows furrowed. His eyes traveled to what was left of the house—her house—and he envisioned her running from pump to house, in the dead of night, and could almost see the flames licking the sky. It had to have been horrible.

He closed his eyes and inhaled deeply, the scent of vanilla from her overtaking that of the ashes before him. How had this slip of a young woman taken care of all of this on her own? It astounded him how that could be possible, and her strength showed in how well the ranch had been cared for. The fire hadn't reached the small garden, and had ruined only part of the barn. The whitewashed boards and neat fences spoke of great pride. No wonder she was devastated that it was all gone. The opportunity to comfort her gave him solace as well. They'd both known loss, but this—on top of losing her parents—would be heart-wrenching.

As she calmed, she lifted her head slowly from his chest and wiped her face with her sleeve before he could reach for his handkerchief. As she pulled away, he handed it to her and his heart lifted at her slight smile.

"I'm sorry," she said as she ran the cloth over her face and turned back to face the wreckage.

He stepped forward, settling his hands on her shoulders. She rested one of her hands on his, and the chill in it rocked him. This all must be quite a shock.

"Please, don't be. This is tragic. *I'm* sorry. Sorry for you and I wish I'd been here to help you," he said, meaning every word of it. She hadn't been his wife at the time, and his mother would have been horrified, but he would have helped. Would have loved to help this woman, even though he had the sense that help wasn't something she needed often.

She offered him a weak smile as she walked toward the pile of belongings under the oak tree that she'd been able to save. She'd borrowed blankets from Joe's house to wrap things up in and he set to helping her pile them onto the fabric, tying up the corners before they lifted them into the back of the buckboard.

There wasn't much to load, actually, and Joe looked over the things she'd chosen to save. There must not have been much time, as it was a few small trinkets—framed photographs, a few pots and pans—and book or two. "How did you decide what to take?" he asked as he lifted a well-worn doll from the pile and placed it on the blanket.

She reached for the doll and held it up, smoothing back the yarn that served for hair on its faded head. "I wasn't thinking. There was no time to think. I was only one step ahead of the flames."

Joe crouched down beside her, fingering the

yellow yarn on the doll. "Looks like you got some important things, anyway," he said as she handed it to him, gratitude in her eyes.

"Baby, meet Joe. Joe, meet baby," she said and he heard the first laugh he'd heard from her since they'd arrived.

"Baby? Not Charlotte or Cassandra?" He took Baby gently from her hands and rested it in her own small blanket, carefully setting her on the seat of the buckboard.

Olivia stood, her eyes following the doll until it was safely situated in the wagon. Her hand rested on her heart as she looked down to the ground and shuffled her feet. "She was a gift when I was a baby myself. I think it's one of the only words I could say at the time, and I never had the heart to change it. So 'Baby' she stayed."

Joe watched as her green eyes softened and she turned back toward the house. "We had many happy times here—well, long ago. But we did."

Joe loaded the last of her things into the back of the wagon. Dust flew as he wiped his hands together and brushed his forehead with his sleeve.

"Do you want to try to take a look in the house? It appears as if one of the rooms was spared. It's a shame that the weather wasn't in your favor. Maybe more could have been saved."

"I don't think there's anything that could have been done," she said, wiping the last tear from her eye. "If there had been, Percy would have gotten ahead of it."

She took a few steps closer to the smokehouse as she squinted, holding her hand over her eyes to shield them from the sun. "When I got here, the fire was in the smokehouse. It hadn't gotten to the house yet. And, I hate to say this, but I tried to enter and—well, I couldn't. The fire was too intense, the smoke billowing everywhere. I just couldn't."

Joe took a few steps toward the smokehouse. "You're thinking of Percy?"

She breathed in deeply and rubbed her forehead. "Yes. He wouldn't have left here, I don't think, and I didn't find..."

Joe's life in town had been pretty staid. Nothing like this happened at the blacksmith shop. The most exciting thing he'd seen was that gunfight between the Earp's and those cowboys, but that had been years ago. He tried his best to keep away from trouble, if he could, especially after what happened to Pa.

Olivia turned back toward the smokehouse, her shoulders squared with determination. "I can't leave until I look in the smokehouse and the barn. I know there wasn't anyone in the house, but I..."

She turned back toward him, beckoning him to follow. He swallowed hard and pulled his hat down more firmly. He'd taken two steps behind her but stopped as a crash sounded from the smokehouse. He took a step back as Olivia turned and ran past him, heading for the buckboard. She jumped on the step and leaned over into the back.

"Oh, my goodness! My shotgun!" Olivia lifted the blankets in the back of the buckboard.

"It—it's not there," he shouted at her as she flung aside the things they'd carefully placed in the wagon.

"What?" she cried as her eyes darted from the wagon to the smokehouse. "You went back to the shop for it this morning."

"I thought about it, but reckoned we'd only be out for the day. It's stowed away tight. Not even Will would be able to find it. If Ma knew—"

Olivia strode toward him, her hands on her hips. "We shouldn't even be out here without a gun. Why, if I'd known, I—"

Another crash came from the smokehouse as several of the boards, almost completely ash, fell in, the roof following.

Olivia ran toward the smokehouse at breakneck

speed, her skirts flying. He threw off his jacket and followed.

Joe raced to keep up with Olivia and couldn't catch her, even though she reached down to pick up a pair of leather gloves and thrown a pair at him, too. She pulled them on as she ran, shouting over her shoulder, "It could be Percy."

She never slowed until she reached the smokehouse, pulling up her sleeves a bit before she grabbed what used to be the doors, he presumed and pulled.

"Wait, let me help you," he said as he tried to nudge her aside.

She wasn't having any of that and stood her ground, tugging as hard as she could until the remnants of the latch fell to the ground and the doors fell—almost directly onto *her*.

He breathed hard and pulled down the other door, grabbing for her arm as she stepped inside. There wasn't much roof left, but the walls were badly burned and unsteady. They'd already watched two of the walls fall, and he tried to pull her back.

"Olivia, I don't think you should—"

She pulled her arm away, her eyes flashing as she turned toward him. "Joe, Percy might be in here and there's nothing that can stop me. If I was here alone, there wouldn't *be* anyone to stop me."

His eyebrows rose and he released his hand. He'd only known this woman mere days, but he cared for her deeply. He wrestled with the desire to keep her safe and the need to—well, make her happy. And she was bound and determined to look for this Percy fellow.

He inhaled deeply and pushed the memory of his father out of his mind.

Holding his arm over his mouth against the billowing ash, just as Olivia did, he followed her through the smokehouse. She lifted and threw boards aside and kicked piles of ashes, calling Percy's name as she worked her way through.

They both breathed deeply of the fresh air as they hopped over the threshold of what had been the back door. Joe wiped his forehead with the back of his hand and leaned down on his knees.

He looked up, surprised to see Olivia staring at the smokehouse, her arms crossed over her chest. She squinted, and craned her neck to peer back inside once or twice before she turned to him, her brows furrowed.

"What is it?" he said when he'd caught his breath.

He stood and rolled his shoulders. "I didn't see anything."

"Exactly," she said as she tapped her finger against her jaw. "I was hoping to find Percy, but glad we didn't, actually."

"What's the problem, then? That should be good news."

Her hands dropped to her hips and she turned back to the smokehouse. "There's nothing there. With all of the hams and bacon inside, it should smell like an outdoor supper over a fire. Nothing. Just burned wood."

"You mean—"

She spun again. "Not even any smoking equipment. No smokers, no metal, no packaging equipment, no branding irons. It's all gone. Many things were metal. They'd be burnt, but they'd be there."

Joe frowned, not quite understanding. He cocked his head and looked at her quizzically.

"It seems everything was gone before the fire. And with Percy missing—it's all very strange.."

CHAPTER 26

The sun was straight overhead when they decided it was time to leave. They'd searched the barn for Percy, as well, and their calls had echoed in the empty, damaged building. Joe had wandered a bit, fingering the neat row of tools hung on the wall and the evenly hammered horseshoes hanging beside them. He'd complimented Olivia on their quality and had been stunned into silence when she'd said, "Thank you. I think I did a nice job of it, too. Pa taught me."

The wagon bounced along, back through the stream bed and Joe shook his head. This woman was like none he'd ever met, and as her head rested on his shoulder—she'd fallen asleep soon after they'd eaten the delicious lunch she'd packed and left the ranch—he wondered if maybe their match had been destined. He'd met lots of fancy women in town—and some rough ones—but she was just in between. Brave but considerate. Kind, but knew what she wanted.

After their trip today, he felt like he knew her better and although he worried for her safety—she didn't seem to be timid at all and certainly knew her mind—he admired her courage. And her commitment to people she loved.

He glanced down at Olivia, her dark lashes resting on her smooth cheeks and he smiled. They began to flutter, and in moments, she was fully awake, her green eyes smiling up at him.

"Goodness, I've been asleep a long time, I see. We're near the outskirts of town already," she said as she took off her bonnet. She took the pins from her hair and ran her fingers through it, twisting it again and replacing the pins. As she re-tied her bonnet, she glanced up at him and her cheeks turned a lovely shade of crimson.

"Joe, you're staring," she said as she folded her hands in her lap and glanced downward.

"So I am. The scenery on the ride home has been lovely."

She nudged him with her elbow but smiled

broadly, her full lips capturing his attention. As they parted, he wondered what it would be like to kiss her.

He tore his gaze away, content to listen to her gentle laughter, and as Tombstone came into view, he spotted his grandmother's house. He looked from the small, neat bungalow with the white picket fence to his new wife and back again. His grandmother, eyes closed, sat on the porch—her usual spot—and rocked back and forth as she hummed. The vivid colors of her shawl filled him with warmth as always and he made a quick decision.

"Olivia, there's someone very special I'd like you to meet," he said as he nudged the horses off the main road and onto the lane that would end at his grandmother's house. It was filled with warm memories for him, of gingerbread baking, pies on the sill and his small hand in his grandmother's soft, larger one as they walked to the park in town.

As he thought about it, he had none, or very vague, memories of his mother. The ones he had, though, were not tinged with warmth. His mother had not welcomed Olivia, but he had no doubt that his grandmother would, with open arms.

"I'd love to meet her," Olivia said after Joe had told her a bit about his father's mother, including a story or two. "This must be her home," Olivia said, laughing, as the sound of snoring could be heard even over the horses' plodding on the soft dirt.

"Indeed it is, and she must be napping in her chair."

The horses tied to the hitching post in front, Joe's grandmother snorted and sat upright as they set foot on the porch stairs. Olivia covered her smile with her hand as the older woman pulled a beautiful shawl tightly around her and beamed at the sight of Joe.

She reached her hands out toward Olivia and Olivia clasped them and drew forward as she said, "And you must be Olivia, my grandson's new bride." The older woman leaned forward and pecked her on both cheeks before turning to Joe with an exaggerated wink.

Olivia's eyebrows shot up at the contrast between this woman and Joe's mother. "Thank you, ma'am. It's a pleasure to meet you, Mrs..." Olivia said slowly as she glanced at Joe, her eyes questioning.

"Call me Grandma, my dear. You're family now." She patted Olivia's cheek and gestured to the porch swing for them to sit.

"Oh, thank you," Olivia said, her eyes wide.

"My son would love you, too, God rest his soul.

He knew a beautiful woman when he saw one. Not sure how he ended up with—"

"Grandma," Joe admonished as he took Olivia's hand and pulled it through his arm. There was no love lost between his mother and grandmother, but they tried to get along. Even after what had happened with Will, it was this most recent issue—Olivia—that had them at odds again. "Please. We're working hard to settle in at the house. Ma's not taking to it too well, though. Hasn't spoken to Olivia at all."

"I've tried to talk to your daughter, ma'am, but she's a tough nut to crack," Olivia said as she accepted the offered glass of lemonade and sat down on the porch swing.

"My daughter? Harrumph, I say. My son married her, and thank goodness he did or we wouldn't have these darling boys, but she's not my daughter." She settled a glass of lemonade in Joe's hand and patted his cheek as well, smiling as she returned to her rocking chair.

"Do take off your bonnet, my dear. Be comfortable. It's warm outside today. The older I get the colder it seems, even in summer. Why, I—"

Joe sat back in the swing, resting his foot on his knee, and smiled as he listened to his grandmother.

Her brown eyes twinkled, and she was just as sharp as she'd always been.

She stopped suddenly as she looked down the lane, over Joe's shoulder. "What on Earth could that woman want?" his grandmother said under her breath.

Joe and Olivia turned to look down the lane, and Olivia's eyebrows rose when he groaned.

His Aunt Dorothy marched purposefully toward them, her head down as her black skirts and black bonnet swayed in the breeze. The glass of her mourning brooch, with a lock of her deceased husband's hair in it, flashed in the late afternoon sunlight.

"You can't help but wonder why she is still in mourning, don't you think? Every time I see her—or your mother, for that matter—I just shake my head. Give me my shawl any day. Your grandfather and father have both been gone for years and years," she said in Olivia's direction as the widow neared.

His grandmother stood, drawing herself up to her full height—which had to be all of five feet—as his aunt reached the bottom of the porch steps.

"What do you want, Dorothy?" she asked as she drew her shawl around her.

The woman glared at his grandmother, her eyes

flashing as she pounded her cane on the lowest step, the porch vibrating each time she did.

"This is a disgrace, Wilma Stanton, and you know it. Why, to interfere in a family like this is—"

"Excuse me, Dorothy Samson, but it's my family you speak of and I'll have none of this disharmony in my home. What's done is done, and I've had the opportunity to meet the charming woman in the center of the issue. You'd be well to make her acquaintance, lest you want to cause further turmoil."

The Widow Samson's mouth had hung open while Joe's grandmother spoke, and she snapped it shut quickly as she narrowed her eyes at Joe, ignoring Olivia completely.

"Joe, I'll have you know that your mother is distraught. She may be smiling, but it's through tears of grief. How could you do this to her?"

Joe stood and opened his mouth to speak.

His grandmother held up her palm to him and said, "Dorothy, do you mean to her or to *you*? I know all about that Jasmine you had picked out for Joe, and it just won't do. Joe can choose his own bride, for his own reasons."

The Widow Samson blanched and pounded her

cane once more as she turned her steely eyes on Mrs. Stanton.

Joe snuck a look at Olivia, her eyes wide as she watched the exchange. He'd have to explain as soon as he could, and he hoped she didn't feel responsible in any way. His family had always been fairly at odds, the reason he and Will had chosen to remain quiet as much of the time as possible. But now, he wanted her to know that they were wrong.

All in all, it had been a good day. He'd admired her greatly, and the Double Barrel Ranch was—or once had been—something mighty fine, with a happy family residing on it. Would that be him, someday? They were already married, of course, but he hoped that someday he could win her heart, and make it truly his. And his aunt standing there, sputtering, made him want it even more.

CHAPTER 27

Joe's Aunt Dorothy certainly had been formidable, and Olivia had felt like a rabbit in a gun sight the entire time she'd been there. She hadn't known any of these things...about how Joe's grandmother felt toward his mother, that his mother had been so very upset about their marriage or that the Widow Samson had already had a bride chosen for Joe.

The widow had stormed off and they'd taken their leave of his grandmother as the sun began to set. They needed to get closer to town before dark, and as Joe kissed his grandmother on the cheek and bid her goodbye, Mrs. Stanton waved and apologized to Olivia.

A wave of exhaustion swept over her, something

she was accustomed to at the end of a long work day, but today had been exhausting in a different way. She wasn't ordinarily surrounded by so many people. She found it more challenging than working a full day at the ranch.

As they neared town, she suddenly thought of Sadie and the baby. Joe mentioned that no baby had come yesterday when he got home from the blacksmith shop, but that it still wasn't clear what was going to happen.

"Joe, I know it's late, but would you mind if we stopped in to see Sadie?" She gestured in the direction of Sadie's house which was directly on the way to their own.

Joe rolled his shoulders back and rubbed the back of his neck. He looked tired to her, and their day had been rather long and trying.

"Of course, if you don't want to, I can step over tomorrow but I thought maybe there might be a baby to see."

"That's fine with me," Joe said as he nudged the horses in the direction of Sadie and Tripp's house. "If all is well there, I might take a quick trip over to the blacksmith shop and see how things went today. You wouldn't mind, would you?"

"No, not at all," Olivia said.

THE BLACKSMITH'S MAIL ORDER BRIDE

Several buggies dotted the drive to Sadie's house. Olivia's stomach clenched at the thought of what she might have missed. Living out on the ranch, she hadn't had much occasion to see or hold a real baby. Hawks, goats and calves—yes—but not a real live human baby.

Joe tied up the buggy and came around, helping Olivia step down. "Would you like to come in?" she asked.

Joe looked around at the buggies. "I'm not much for big crowds," he said as he shifted his weight from boot to boot. "Why don't you go in and see what's going on? It might be that they're not prepared for many more people than they already seem to have."

Olivia nodded and untied her bonnet, shaking off some of the dirt of the day. "I won't be a minute," she said as Joe turned, touching the brim of his hat and nodding before he headed toward the blacksmith shop.

Olivia climbed the steps of the porch, nodding her head toward the door before she knocked. It wasn't always good things that happened when babies were coming, and she didn't want to interrupt.

Laughter tumbled through the open kitchen window, and she took a deep breath. Certainly that was a good sign. As she lifted her hand to knock, the door opened, Suzanne smiling broadly at her. Olivia smiled herself as her friend grabbed her hand and pulled her inside.

"Olivia, I'm so glad to see you. You left in such a hurry the other night."

She hung her hat quickly on the hook by the door as she pulled her inside the kitchen, pushing the door open and letting it swing closed behind them.

Olivia stopped in her tracks at the sight of Sadie sitting at the table, a cup of tea poised in midair. She quickly looked down to Sadie's belly — it was as big as the night she'd left.

"False alarm," Sadie said as she rubbed her hand over her apron. Her eyes twinkled as she looked up at her husband.

Tripp leaned against the counter and shook his head. "This baby sure is giving us a run for our money." He crossed over to Sadie and placed his hands on her shoulders.

Sadie rested her cheek on his hand. "I would have to agree with you on that count. But we all know the baby wasn't supposed to come yet, so it's a blessing."

Suzanne wiped her forehead with the back of her hand in an exaggerated sigh of relief. "It was quite nerve-racking there for a little bit, but it was a good thing Sage was here. She has such a level head. Had she not been here, I don't know what we would have done when the doctor never arrived."

"Yes, it certainly was helpful that she was available." Tripp frowned as he ran his hand through his hair. He exchanged a quick glance with Suzanne, but his smile returned as he sat down in the chair beside Sadie.

"Would you care for a cup of tea?" Suzanne asked Olivia. "Things are much calmer this evening and would love for you to stay a bit. How have things been at your new home?"

Olivia took the cup and saucer of steaming tea that Suzanne held out to her. She sat down slowly in the chair that Suzanne gestured to, reaching for a spoon and placing two teaspoons of sugar in her tea.

"Olivia?" Sadie asked as she leaned forward. "Is anything wrong?"

Olivia certainly didn't want to rain on their parade. After all, it had been Suzanne and Sadie who'd convinced her to marry Joe in the first place. And she certainly couldn't complain about Joe. He'd been quite helpful on the trip out to the ranch, even if he had left her shotgun behind.

She shared the events of the day with them, especially the perplexing information that all of her inventory has disappeared, even the equipment.

"You mean you think it might have been stolen?"

She shook her head slowly. "I don't really know. Joe and I looked for Percy, but couldn't find a thing. From what I could tell, most of his clothes were still there, along with his personal belongings. I can't imagine he would have stolen it all and run."

"But you're positive that the inventory didn't just burn with the fire?" Suzanne said as she stood and paced the kitchen floor.

"Fairly. I can't be certain, but there was no trace of our equipment or packaging. And there wasn't an overwhelming scent of burning bacon," she said with a weak smile.

Suzanne rested her hand on Olivia's shoulder. "This must all be awful for you. I'm so sorry for all your trouble—with Joe's mother, also."

"I'm still hoping that everything will work out," Olivia said as she stood. "I know that I'm not exactly what Joe's mother hoped for. We do come from very different worlds."

While she'd been stunned that he had taken both of them all the way out to the Double Barrel Ranch without – well, without a double-barreled shotgun, she couldn't blame him, really. With the agreement made about no guns in the blacksmith shop, and the fact that he lived in town, he wouldn't understand how important it would be to have protection out in such a wild place at the ranch.

She didn't want to worry her friends. They'd vouched for her with Joe, and salvaged what was a really bad situation.

But what she'd heard from his aunt, combined with the response she received from his mother, had shaken her. How would she be able to live in a home with someone who refused to acknowledge her, let alone speak with her?

Suzanne's voice pulled her from her thoughts. "Olivia?" Suzanne said as she looked from Sadie to Tripp. "You know, if you haven't consummated the marriage, it could be annulled."

Olivia's eyes flew open wide and heat crept up her neck. "Oh, goodness. I—well, there's not been—oh, I don't want an annulment."

Suzanne's eyes sparkled. "You have feelings for Joe?" she asked, her hand resting on Olivia's.

Olivia's cheeks bloomed to full crimson as the thought of being without Joe knotted her stomach. She hadn't known him long, but he'd been very kind and she'd grown accustomed to his laugh.

But the memory of the worry lines that creased

his forehead each time they spoke of his mother troubled her.

"I do," she said finally. "I'll just do my best to make her happy."

"His mother?" Sadie said with a frown as she shook her head. "She's not warmed up to Carol. I think that may be a tough row to hoe."

Olivia stood and squared her shoulders. "I'm going to give it my best. She might come around. Although after speaking with his aunt today, it may take a little longer than I'd hoped."

Sadie and Suzanne exchanged quick glances. "Oh, that woman!" Suzanne exclaimed. "Olivia, I applaud your resolve, but please know we are here if you need us."

CHAPTER 28

Silence roared through the dining room as it had each and every evening for the days Olivia had been married. In the beginning, she'd tried to make conversation with her new mother-in-law but her queries seemed to fall on deaf ears. Not only had Mrs. Stanton not replied, she'd begun to even avoid looking at either her son or her new daughter-in-law.

No matter that Olivia had tried her best to create suppers using the wonderful vegetables that were placed in a bowl on the kitchen counter after Mrs. Stanton had spent the day in her beloved garden. Even the compliments on her fresh tomatoes this evening, which she and Joe ooh-ed and aah-ed over

—they really were delicious, so fresh and flavorful—had been met with no response.

During the days while Joe was at the shop, she'd busied herself in the kitchen, making herself familiar with the supplies and sometimes heading to the mercantile to fetch something she needed. Each and every time, Suzanne asked, "Has she spoken to you yet?" And each time Olivia had shaken her head slowly.

There had only been three of them for the most part on the ranch as she grew up, but it had been much more lively than this. She'd enjoyed reading to her parents in the evening, after the sun had set, as they sat by the wood stove. At least she and Joe had taken that up, and she spent her days looking forward to that time in the evenings.

After a few days, she'd explored every inch of the house, all while sneaking peeks at Mrs. Stanton. If she wasn't tending to her garden, she was in her room—presumably reading. Her heart ached to sit down to a cup of tea with her and find out more about Joe, more about the family, but she'd stopped hoping days ago.

The silence was getting to her. At least at the ranch she'd been out all day with tasks to accomplish. And in the final years, she'd had Percy—he wasn't good for much, but he was always ready with a good joke. Her heart ached for human contact—irony that wasn't lost on her. She'd agreed to come to town fearing it might be too *much* for her. Strange that it wasn't enough.

After yet another silent supper, Olivia cleared the table, glancing up at her mother-in-law as she swept from the room. She peeked out the door off the dining room and her heart pinched as Mrs. Stanton's bedroom door closed with a thud.

She'd tried everything she could think of. She'd asked about the weather. She'd asked about her garden. She'd asked about Joe but each and every time had been met with a wall of chilly silence.

Lightning flashed through the parlor windows as Olivia settled in what had become her armchair—at least it had in her thoughts. Too warm for a fire, she opened the window and looked at the flashes in the distance. The squall would be there soon, but for now, the scent of the coming rain cleared her head.

She'd learned that Joe wasn't the most talkative man in the world, either, but he'd always chatted with her in the evenings.

"How is everything at the blacksmith shop, Joe?" She hungered for information about anything in the world other than how much flour was in the larder.

"Things have been busy. Very busy, actually."

Olivia looked up from her project, just noticing that she'd gotten her stitches off yet again. It wasn't exactly something she enjoyed or was very good at, but it was better than nothing at all.

"Oh? Even with both of you there? You and Will?"

"Yes, even with us both. And Will informed me today that he's leaving with Carol for Tucson. They've got an appointment with a doctor."

"Oh, not a doctor here in town?"

Joe glanced quickly up at her. "I'm not sure, but I believe there's a reason they wish to see another, different doctor."

Olivia's eyebrows rose as she recalled that the doctor hadn't arrived at Sadie's house when needed.

"Is she all right?" she said as she frowned. She glanced at Joe and his brows were furrowed as well.

"Yes, I'm sure she is. I am worried about all the work we have to do, though. Not sure how I'll manage on my own."

Olivia's heart about leaped into her throat. She glanced at the horrible cross stitching she'd done and her hands grew damp.

"Joe?" she said as she stood and crossed the room, taking a seat beside him on the settee. "You know, I have a lot of experience fixing things. I ran the ranch virtually on my own. I'd love to help."

Joe set the book he'd been reading on his lap and met her eyes. "I don't think that would be a good idea, Olivia. It's dangerous in there. Many things could go wrong, and—"

"Joe, that's nonsense. What could happen in the shop that hasn't happened out on the ranch? We had unexpected things come up all the time and we had to make do."

"Make do is right, but you haven't been trained..."

Joe pulled at his collar as he averted his eyes.

"You said yourself that the horseshoes I'd made were some of the best you'd ever seen," she said, raising her eyebrows at him as she pulled his chin toward her, forcing him to meet her gaze. She couldn't bear one more moment in this silent house, and he knew she was good enough to help in the shop. It would be a change for him, but she just had to get out and be useful.

"Well, I suppose it would be only temporary. Will expects to be gone only for a week. I imagine we could give it a try. If you'll just keep to the simple things, it might help a great deal."

Simple things? Olivia had spent very little time in the shop but had no doubt whatsoever that she would be able to do much more than simple things. Joe still sounded a little unsure, so she chose to keep her plans to herself.

Maybe this was just the solution she'd been looking for. She'd get to the shop, show him how much she could do and would never have to spend an entire day in this silent house alone again.

CHAPTER 29

Olivia straightened the sheets that had been crumpled at her feet when she'd awoken after a night of tossing and turning. The cause had not been worry but excitement, and she hopped out of bed at the first touch of orange light through her bedroom window.

She made coffee for Joe and herself, taking care to set a cup on the table for her mother-in-law. When Mrs. Stanton came in for a cup of coffee and never even looked in Olivia's direction, her decision was confirmed. She couldn't wait to get out of this house.

She glanced back over her shoulder once as Joe steered the buggy toward the blacksmith shop. Mrs.

Stanton was in her usual position, bonnet intact as she reached over the chicken wire to pull weeds from her garden. Olivia's heart sang as she turned and looked forward to her day.

The morning rushed by as Joe took time to explain things to Olivia. She had paid close attention and wanted to jump right into helping, as much as he would let her. She was bound and determined to prove her value in the blacksmith shop.

Joe reached for his leather apron after showing her around the shop, but hesitated a moment. "Oh, I forgot. I'm expecting a parcel at the mercantile. Suzanne ordered some nails for me, a new type that is advertised as non-rusting. I'll run over and pick them up," he said as he reached for his hat.

"Oh, might I go, Joe? I would be pleased to see Suzanne again, and it might be that someone's heard something about the ranch." Her eyes clouded at the memory of the empty smokehouse. "I still don't know what happened to all the inventory. Or Percy."

Joe nodded and reached for his apron instead. "All right. That's fine. I'll start on these horseshoes, then."

Olivia smiled and reached for her bonnet. As Joe tied his leather apron behind his back and reached for his iron tongs, she looked about the room. The small shop could use a bit of tidying up—it was obviously the domain of men—and she was pleased that she could do that for them. They'd make a good team.

"I'll be back shortly," she said over her shoulder as she gave him her best smile.

The clock struck ten as she hurried down the boardwalk—as quickly as she could as she was jostled by people doing the same. The mines ran around the clock, seven days a week, and the town had grown so quickly that the boardwalk was crowded, even at this time of the morning.

She'd spent so little time in town that this was a surprise to her. Men and women, arm in arm, strolled past restaurants she'd never noticed before, feathers plumed on their hats just as she'd imagined. Schoolchildren, their mornings free now it was summer, scurried between buildings with puppies running quickly behind them.

She stepped off of the boardwalk to cross the street, distracted by the sign for the bowling alley further down the street. Young ladies blushed as they ducked in, young men close behind them. She'd been told that the theaters and bowling alley, even the ice cream parlor, were open odd hours, due to the miners unusual working hours, and she shook her head. Before, she'd found all this activity annoying, and had tried to avoid it. Now that her life was here, she found it oddly invigorating. Maybe Joe would take her to the bowling alley one evening. She'd love to see it.

Tombstone had changed a great deal and she hadn't even noticed, so far out at the ranch.

She looked up, welcoming the warm sun on her skin as she hurried across the busy street. Mud puddles from the evening before stood scattered across the dirt road and the shout of a carriage driver brought her attention back to the ground. At the corner, a well-dressed man unbuttoned his cape and threw it over a puddle for a woman in a fancy hat and velvet dress. She shook her head at something so silly. The carriage driver shouted again, and she stepped back to let him pass and jumped over the puddle before her, scurrying up the steps to the mercantile as quickly as she could.

The mercantile was equally crowded, and Olivia paused in the doorway. She scouted the aisles for Suzanne and spotted her in the back, talking to a man in a tall black hat. She approached, but held back until Suzanne was finished with her conversation.

As she waited, she fingered her reticule and browsed the aisles. Suzanne and James had opened the mercantile long ago, when Tombstone had been much smaller. They'd designed it the common way, in the beginning, and customers had given them a list of things they wanted to purchase. They'd gathered items individually from behind a counter but now, items were in the center of the shop, and customers gathered their own items in baskets. Olivia marveled at the changes she'd missed.

Next to her, a lovely woman stood at the counter. Her gentle, lavender perfume had caused Olivia to look up before she'd even seen her, and she was struck by her elegance, even at ten o'clock in the morning. Her dress was impeccable, and her hat matched perfectly—a stunning color that matched her eyes. In her hand, she held a pearl-handled revolver. Her brows furrowed as she turned it over in her hands. She looked up and cast her glance about the mercantile. Her eyes eventually settled on Olivia, who was admiring the beautiful pistol.

"That's a lovely piece of work," Olivia said as she admired the pistol. The mother of pearl inlay was clearly quite expensive.

"Thank you," the woman said in a smooth, calming voice. "It was my mother's and is very dear to me. I'm Helen Allen," she said as she extended her gloved hand toward Olivia with a sparkling smile.

Olivia shook her hand and nodded. "Olivia. Olivia Blanch—Stanton," she said, returning the older woman's smile. Her black hair had the finest streaks of gray and was pinned elegantly, a few curling tendrils framing her face.

"Oh, it's very nice to meet you. You're the young lady who married that charming blacksmith."

Olivia's heart swelled at the mention of Joe. "Yes, I did. I was quite fortunate in that circumstance," she said and shared with Mrs. Allen briefly the particulars of their nuptials as she waited for Suzanne.

"Goodness, what an adventure," Mrs. Allen said as she rested her hand on her chest. "I do hope all ends well for you, my dear."

"Thank you," Olivia said as she glanced at Suzanne. She and the man were still talking, and Olivia turned back to Mrs. Allen.

She turned her attention back to the gun. "I do wish I could ascertain what is wrong with this, however."

"May I?" Olivia asked as she held her hand out

toward the gun. She'd never seen such a lovely pistol, one so delicate.

"Of course," Mrs. Allen said as she smiled and placed the gun in Olivia's palm. "It's quite old, and as I said it was my mother's. I'd be quite pleased if it worked properly."

Olivia's eyebrows rose as she glanced up toward Mrs. Allen and wondered what she might need with a pistol. In her experience, though, she knew there could be many reasons and decided not to ask.

She moved her hands quickly as she eyed the steel. With a few quick motions, she clicked the hammer back into place and smiled. "That should do it, I believe." She handed the gun back to Mrs. Allen who beamed at her broadly.

"Oh, goodness! Thank you. My mother will be so pleased. Mr. Archer, however, may not be."

"Mr. Archer?" Olivia asked as she picked up her reticule from the counter where she'd set it.

"Yes, a friend," Mrs. Allen said as she inspected the unloaded gun. She placed it in her reticule and said, "I look forward to trying it, my dear. Thank you."

Olivia nodded and glanced back at Suzanne. The man she'd been speaking to had turned toward the door and Suzanne frowned as she watched him walk away.

"Thank you, sir," Suzanne said as she took a piece of paper from the man she'd been talking to. He doffed his hat and left through the back door, stepping up into the front of a buckboard. He nodded again as he nudged his horses down the road, and Olivia's mouth dried at the letters painted on the side—Tucson Pork Delivery.

Suzanne turned as she frowned down at the paper in her hand. She bumped into Olivia and looked up, startled.

"Suzanne?" Olivia asked, her hands damp. "Who was that?"

The man drove away as Suzanne shoved the paper in her pocket. "Nobody. I mean, I don't know. Yet. I'll let you know when he comes back with a sample."

"I would love to hear more about the ranch, my dear. It is quite unusual to have a fire and lose an entire inventory in such a manner. Is there no indication that there was a theft?" Mrs. Allen said as she stepped over to where Olivia and Suzanne watched the delivery wagon disappear down the dirt road.

Olivia frowned and ran the particulars through her mind once more from when she and Joe had searched the smokehouse. "I really didn't think of it at the time. It did appear that everything was missing, but I don't think I have any way of knowing for sure."

"Ah, young lady, there is always a way to tell. People leave clues, and clues can be found. Always," Mrs. Allen said as she nodded knowingly at Olivia.

CHAPTER 30

The knot in Olivia's stomach had eased by the time she got back to the shop with Joe's package. Was it, in fact, her ham that the stranger was trying to sell to Suzanne? She couldn't imagine it would be—they were branded, after all. The hams and slabs of bacon as well. It would be simple to tell if it was, and she was certain that when the man brought one back, it would all be resolved.

The question of Percy, though, still ran through her mind. Nobody could sell the inventory without it being identifiable as belonging to the Double Barrel Ranch, so what happened to Percy? It wouldn't be the first time a ranch hand disappeared, likely with a better offer, and she pushed the thought from her mind.

Joe stopped hammering as she told the story of what she'd learned. He'd set his tongs down and sat on the stool beside her.

"Does she have any reason to believe that it's from your ranch?" he'd asked slowly as she finished.

"Not exactly."

"Why is she suspicious?" he asked, his arms folded across his chest.

Olivia stood and began to pace. "I'm not certain. She mentioned she'd never seen him before although he mentioned they'd been in business in Tucson for some time. He's bringing a sample back for her to assess, and then she might know."

"Nothing to do then, but wait until he does," Joe said slowly.

"And that should be soon, I'd guess," Olivia said as she sat back down at the desk, only to stand again as the bells on the door jingled and Mrs. Allen stepped inside.

"Mrs. Allen. What a nice surprise," Joe said as he smiled and nodded in her direction.

"Nice to see you, too, Joe. I stopped to compliment your wife on her skills. She fixed my gun in minutes, and it hasn't worked in ages."

Joe's smile quickly faded as his eyes locked on the pearl-handled revolver in Mrs. Allen's hands.

"She fixed your gun?" he said, his eyes traveling from the gun to Olivia.

Olivia's smile faded, too, at his tone and a shadow of confusion passed over Mrs. Allen's lovely face.

"Oh. I'm sorry, Joe. I forgot we're not supposed to fix guns," Olivia said slowly as she looked down at her boots.

"Whyever not?" Mrs. Allen asked as she looked back and forth between the two of them. "Your lovely wife is gifted—at more than gunsmithing, I'd venture to guess." She winked at Olivia as she placed the gun back in her reticule and pulled out some coins. "I came to pay you for your trouble. It's been years since I've been able to use it."

She held out the coins, her eyebrows raised expectantly for them to take the money.

Joe stood and held his palms out toward her. "No, Mrs. Allen, we couldn't possibly. We don't service guns in the shop—I do apologize, and it's a long story. But I can't—we can't."

"Don't be silly. I insist," she said as she winked at Olivia and nodded, placing the coins on the desk. "For services rendered. Thank you again, my dear," she said as she breezed back out the door as quickly as she'd entered.

Olivia stared at the coins on the desk and looked

up at Joe, her eyes questioning. It had been a quick decision on her part—something that was simple to do and Mrs. Allen needed done.

Joe groaned as he looked out the window onto Allen Street and Olivia followed his gaze.

Mrs. Allen chatted with Joe's aunt, the Widow Samson and tapped her reticule. "Good grief. I hope she..."

Olivia sat as he paused. "Are they not friends?" Olivia asked.

Joe frowned as he turned back toward Olivia. "I'm not sure anyone is a friend of my aunt's, except my mother," he said as he paced for a few moments.

Olivia watched out the window as Mrs. Allen and the Widow Samson concluded their conversations and parted ways.

As her thoughts turned back to the inventory and Suzanne's suspicions, she was grateful for the busywork that the blacksmith had to offer.

Joe had eventually donned his heavy leather apron and set to fixing an iron gate he'd been working on. He asked Olivia to sort through some hardware, separating nails and things of different sizes on the workbench. She didn't mind at all. Anything was better than wandering an empty house and certainly better than attempting to cross stitch.

The rhythm of Joe's hammer soothed her, and she thought that there was no place else she'd rather be.

In her excitement, she'd forgotten to bring anything for them to eat. As the clock by the door struck noon, Joe's stomach rumbled. He looked up at her hopefully.

She jumped up from her stool at the hardware bench, hastily removing the apron he'd given her.

"Joe, I'm so sorry. I was so excited to come with you today that I completely forgot to prepare lunch for us. I can run home and get something and bring it back," she said as she reached for her bonnet by the door.

Joe set down the long iron tongs he'd been using to pull horseshoes from the bucket in front of him. He reached for a cloth to the side and wiped his hands clean. "I can go with you, Olivia. I know you don't want to be alone with Ma."

He and Olivia hadn't discussed her discontent much. She'd kept her concerns to herself, except for the occasional comment to Sadie or Suzanne. The last thing she wanted was to come between Joe and his mother, but if she'd actually cast Will out she wasn't sure what she could do.

But she was going to keep trying. If she ran home, maybe she could make something for Mrs. Stanton, too. It certainly couldn't hurt. It couldn't possibly get any worse than it already was.

She crossed over to Joe. "I'm sorry that I haven't been able to bring her around, Joe. I've tried everything I can think of and nothing's helped."

Sorrow filled his eyes as he looked down at her. "I know, Olivia. It's not you. It's Ma—she's just not been the same since Pa died. I thought that maybe she'd warm up, take a shine to you. I know I certainly have."

Olivia's breath hitched in her throat at his words. She'd grown quite fond of him as well in the time they'd been wed, and in the evenings, she was now sorry that they had to part. Maybe if she could figure out a way to bring Mrs. Stanton around they could be a real couple—a real family.

She covered Joe's palm with hers as he rested it on her cheek. She closed her eyes, feeling the warmth and comfort spread from him. Yes, that was what she wanted. And she would do whatever she had to to make that happen.

Maybe going home and making lunch for the

three of them was just the ticket. And maybe, if Suzanne was able to identify her inventory and she could get it back—and the money it would bring—they could re-build the ranch and have both the ranch and the blacksmith shop. A perfect life.

She opened her eyes and looked up into the depths of Joe's soft brown ones.

Yes, she'd do whatever she needed to do to make Joe happy—and have the life she'd dreamed of.

CHAPTER 31

She hummed a tune as she walked back toward the house. The beautiful summer afternoon begged for a walk, the crystal blue growing darker with billowing clouds, heavy with rain. But it wasn't raining yet, and the warm sun buoyed her spirits. The dust had settled as she left Allen Street and turned north, passing small, well-kept houses on each side. Curtains billowed through open windows in the breeze. Quiet descended as she approached the outskirts of town, the hustle and bustle far behind.

Her thoughts turned to Mrs. Stanton. Joe had said she was different before his father died. And he'd yet to tell her what had actually happened, other than he'd been killed in an accident. But this family certainly didn't seem inclined to talk about it much, and she wouldn't be asking. Some things were better left unsaid.

Hope swelled in her heart as she thought of the blacksmith shop and the possibility of finding her inventory—maybe they could even re-build the ranch. Things were turning out better than she'd ever imagined, and she felt a skip in her step as she turned up the road toward the Stanton home. She wondered if it would ever feel like her own, but she was bound and determined to try.

Her heart skipped a beat as she rounded the corner. The buggy was unmistakable—the Widow Samson's. She'd seen it enough times in the past week to recognize it anywhere, its black flag flying from the lantern unique.

She mustered her courage and walked forward. After all, this was her aunt now, too, and along with his mother, she'd do whatever she could to make peace. For Joe's sake.

"You must be joking, Dorothy. That's not possible. Joe would never do such a thing. Not against my wishes, certainly, but knowing the consequences...he would never."

"I'm telling you, I saw it with my own eyes, Lucinda."

Olivia had barely heard her new mother-in-law's voice at all, but was fairly certain that it was she who was speaking with the Widow Samson before she even set foot in the door. The voices had come from the open kitchen window, and she stepped softly closer to it so as to hear what they were saying. She didn't want to take the risk of stepping inside for fear that Mrs. Stanton would stop speaking, and then she'd never know what they were thinking.

"I'm telling you, I saw it. Mrs. Allen even showed me the gun."

Olivia pressed her back to the side of the house at the sound of a chair scraping against the floor.

"Was it something that the ridiculous girl did on her own? Without Joe's knowledge? He knows that I've forbidden the repair of guns in that shop, and he also knows the consequences."

The sound of the Widow Samson's voice grew louder, closer to the window, and Olivia held her breath.

Her cold voice was clear, and Olivia could almost imagine her self-satisfied expression as she said, "He knew. He knew full well."

Mrs. Stanton's voice grew quiet. Olivia strained to hear her.

"There must be some explanation," Joe's mother

said quietly. "Certainly, he wouldn't—I mean, with his father's accident, and knowing how I feel—"

"My dear," Mrs. Swanson said as Olivia crept closer to the window. "It is certain. Mrs. Allen showed me the gun, and told me how much she'd paid."

A moment or two passed and Olivia could only imagine what was going on in the kitchen. Her mouth went dry as Mrs. Stanton finally spoke.

"Well, the decision has been made. By Joe. The shop will be sold."

"Serves him right," the widow added. "He never should have risked it by taking in that creature. All of this sordid business could have been avoided."

A cold chill ran down Olivia's back as she heard the Widow Samson say, "Ah, my dear. It's a perfect opportunity to tell him it's the shop...or his new wife."

Olivia's heart quickened and she feared that it beat so loud they might hear it. What was so wrong with what she'd done? She knew Joe had been upset, and she hadn't wanted to take the money anyway. She was just trying to help, and Mrs. Allen was so kind. He must have known what would happen—he'd asked her not to do it again and she'd agreed. Now, he'd lost the shop and it was all her fault.

The deafening silence crushed Olivia. She slid down the side of the wall and crouched, blood rushing so loudly through her head that she couldn't think. How could this be? With one simple act, she'd lost the shop for Joe and his brother.

She stood, inching up against the wall of the house. Holding her breath, she tiptoed across the porch, away from the window, as quietly as she could. When she reached the far end of the house, she rounded the corner and sunk into a heap again on the floorboards.

She shook her head slowly, trying to gather her wits about her. Tears streamed down her face and her eyes darted along the street as she looked for a place to run.

CHAPTER 32

Joe's stomach grumbled loudly as the clock struck one. He frowned—Olivia had been gone an awfully long time just to grab some food. He'd been reticent to let her go on her own. The troubles with his mother had been getting to both of them, although she didn't speak of it much. He knew it had to be wearing on her, as it was him.

He'd never have guessed his mother would have been so stubborn when he'd decided to marry Olivia. At the time, it seemed like the right thing to do to stay as far away as possible from that horrid woman she wanted him to marry.

Maybe it had been a bit impulsive on his part, searching for a mail order bride and taking Olivia in, but he'd grown quite fond of her. She was beautiful, yes, and each day as he learned more about her, his fondness had grown. Today, he'd placed his hand on her warm cheek and she'd placed her hand on his, he'd wanted to kiss her—badly. Her big heart and kindness were only a few of her appealing qualities—he knew he shouldn't be impressed that she'd fixed Mrs. Allen's gun, but he was.

His lips tugged up into a smile. He'd asked her not to, but she'd done such a good job of it. And so quickly. She knew things he didn't, even though he was the blacksmith, and her skills and courage impressed him. Even when they'd been out at the ranch, she'd had the courage to do things that hadn't even occurred to him.

Courageous as she was, he knew his mother could be a formidable adversary—he only had to look at Will and Carol to see that. They'd actually left and built a new home for themselves rather than accept what he'd been expecting Olivia to put up with.

He shouldn't have let her go on her own, and he quickly took off his apron as his stomach knotted. She should have been back by now. He flipped the sign on the door to "Closed" and hurried off in the direction of the house.

His pace quickened as he crossed through the lanes, oblivious to the warm sun on his skin. He looked up once at the clouds that gathered, dark ones that announced there would be an evening storm. It didn't bother him one way or another, and as he broke into a run he tried to convince himself that everything would be fine. He and Olivia would have lunch and work in the shop, return home for supper and spend a cozy evening watching the rain from inside the parlor. Maybe he'd even light a fire.

Joe unlatched the gate to his home and slid through, his hat pulled down over his head against the coming rain. His stomach dropped at the sight of his aunt's buggy and steeled himself, ready for anything. He stopped short at the bottom of the porch steps as he heard his mother laugh—something he hadn't heard in a long time. It didn't sound mirthful, however, and his breath hitched at what she must be saying to Olivia.

He slammed the door as he entered, heading straight for the kitchen.

"It really couldn't be better, my dear. Joe will never agree to selling the shop, and it's the perfect solution."

He tossed his hat on the hook and stopped for a moment, his eyes closed as the voice of his aunt sunk deep into his bones. He never should have let her come alone. Now she was at the mercy of two of them—his mother *and* his aunt.

They both stood as he pushed through the door, his eyes darting around the kitchen in search of his wife.

"Where is Olivia?" he blurted, taking a step further into the kitchen.

"Well, that's a fine greeting," his aunt said. She looked like a cat who'd swallowed a canary, and her hands rested on her large stomach. She lifted a brow and glanced at his mother, a similar expression on her face.

"Sit down, Joe. I have something to tell you," his mother said, the most words he'd heard from her since he'd been married.

"I don't want to sit. Where is Olivia?" he asked again as he struggled to stand still.

"I have no idea where your bride is." Her words dripped icily as her smile turned smug. "And I don't believe I'll be seeing her again with what I have to impart."

"What do you mean?" he asked, his hands clenching at his sides. He closed his eyes, unable to imagine what she was talking about. Not see Olivia again? Certainly, tonight, for supper...

She sat at the kitchen table and folded her hands in her lap. "Suit yourself. Your aunt informs me that you have disregarded my request and accepted the repair of a gun in the shop. You know it is against my wishes that you do so."

Joe frowned and glared at his aunt. Of course she would have reported what she'd seen with haste. "Olivia didn't know. She did it out of the shop, anyway."

"Is it not true that she was paid for her services? At the shop?" his aunt added, her smile as smug as his mother's.

Joe tugged at his collar and tore his hands through his hair. "It was all a misunderstanding. Olivia didn't mean to..."

Mrs. Stanton raised an eyebrow and smiled. Joe wished he could explain. He'd tried to tell Olivia, and he thought she understood now, but the damage had been done. He knew any argument would fall on deaf ears, certainly with these two.

"I've made my decision, Joe. The shop will be sold. It shouldn't be a surprise to you."

The air rushed out of his chest as he looked from his mother to his aunt, appalled at the satisfaction on their faces. How could they think this was a good solution?

The Widow Samson strummed her fingernails on the table, barely able to hide her glee. "Well, you did have a suitable alternative. Didn't you, my dear?"

"Oh, thank you for reminding me," his mother said as she turned toward Joe. The malicious twinkle in her eye nauseated him, and he braced himself for what she might say.

"I would reconsider, of course, if you agree to return that wretched creature back from whence she came."

She drew out every word as he blanched, hardly believing his ears.

"Wretched creature? Olivia?" he said when he'd found his voice, his blood pounding in his ears. Who in their right mind could ever speak of Olivia so? His eyes widened in horror at the woman his mother had become, grateful his father wasn't present. It would break his heart.

But he refused his own to be broken. He squared his shoulders and reached into his pocket. Would Will agree? He was certain he would—he loved Carol as much as Joe loved Olivia.

Loved Olivia? Warmth flooded through him as he realized that he did. And that he would do anything to protect her—unfortunately, from his own flesh and blood. But so be it.

He reached into the pocket of his waistcoat, fingering the cool metal. He knew his father would approve, and his hand grew tight around what had been in his pocket every day for a decade. Longer, if he counted the days he followed his father into the shop, close on his heels as they laughed and planned their day.

His mother and aunt's eyes grew wide and they pursed their lips in unison as he dropped the key to the blacksmith shop on the table before them. It settled with a thud after it had spun for a second, Joe's eyes twinkling at his immediate rush of freedom.

"Joe, you can't—"

"I certainly can, Mother, and I have. I wish you the best running the shop on your own, or selling it as you see fit. I'm through."

He smiled, feeling lighter than he had in years and years. Well, he couldn't even remember when he'd felt so free.

He turned on his heels and grabbed his hat. He strode onto the porch and took in a deep breath, the air threatening rain. But he didn't care. He needed to find Olivia. His wife.

CHAPTER 33

Olivia ran blindly through her tears, not exactly clear where she was heading. Once again, she'd found herself with nothing but the clothes on her back—not even her gun, at Joe's request—or her buggy and horses that were still at the livery.

Her steps slowed when she realized she was far enough away from those two women, and she struggled to keep unkind thoughts from her head. How could they possibly think it was in anyone's best interest to sell the shop? Joe would have nothing, Will would have nothing, and the thought of them no longer working in the shop that they'd built with their father—well, it was more than she could bear.

She couldn't allow it. Joe couldn't lose the shop, and she'd heard Mrs. Stanton say that if she herself was out of the picture, she'd let him stay. And that's what needed to happen.

She rested her hands on her knees as she caught her breath, ignoring two women who tittered as they passed by, their heads close together.

She shook her head, irritated. This town certainly wasn't for her, it seemed. Nobody tittered at her on the ranch. There wasn't anyone there *to* titter, and while she'd been enamored with all the bright, shiny people when she'd first arrived, all she wanted now was quiet and solitude. And the ranch was the only place she could think of to find it.

Her mind raced at the thought. Maybe Suzanne had found her inventory, and she would get paid for it after all. After she proved it was hers, unfortunately. In truth, she had nowhere else to go, so whether or not she got paid for the inventory, the ranch was where she'd have to head.

When she and Joe had searched the property, the barn hadn't been completely demolished by the fire. She could stay in Percy's quarters until she figured out what to do. Unless, of course, he'd returned, but she'd have to deal with that when—or if—that was the case.

THE BLACKSMITH'S MAIL ORDER BRIDE

Her breath had returned fully, and she looked up and turned full circle, getting her bearings. In her despair, she'd actually run closer to town and she headed in the direction of the mercantile, skirting the edge on the side streets so as not to require passing in front of the blacksmith shop.

She quickly breezed by an alleyway but couldn't help take a glance at the window of the blacksmith shop as she snuck by. Joe would be even hungrier by now, and her heart grew heavy at the thought that she would no longer be able to cook for him, see him smile as she read to him, or even hear him laugh at her paltry cross stitch efforts.

She shook off the thought as her eyes lit on the sign in front of the shop. "Stanton and Sons." She couldn't allow him to lose everything he'd worked for, everything he loved—because of her.

She shivered as lightning flashed and she pulled her bonnet down over her eyes. Thunder rolled in the distance, toward the west and the Double Barrel Ranch. At least she and Percy had re-done the roof of the barn last winter, and that would hold, long enough anyway for her to figure out what to do.

As she approached the back door of the mercantile, she ducked around the corner as a wagon departed—the same pork wagon she'd seen earlier.

Suzanne held a package in her hands and frowned as the driver nudged his horses down the lane. She studied the package for a moment and turned back in to the mercantile.

Olivia ran up the stairs and followed. "Suzanne?"

Suzanne turned suddenly, concern shadowing her face.

"Oh, Olivia. Just the person I wanted to see," she said as she gestured for Olivia to follow her into the mercantile office. "He brought back the sample."

Suzanne set down the package, something wrapped in brown paper and tied with twine. Suzanne reached for the letter opener and cut the twine, quickly unwrapping the package.

She swiftly pushed aside the paper, and turned over what Olivia recognized as a ham. Her stomach sunk as she moved aside the remaining wrapper and gasped as she saw the branding on the side.

"Your brand was DBR. This is BBB," Suzanne said as she shook her head slowly.

It wasn't her exact brand, but she was sure it had been—and branded over to look like a different one. The DBR that her pa had insisted they branded onto the hams had changed to BBB.

"Suzanne, it's—it wouldn't be difficult to brand

over the DBR lettering. Should have made something fancier, but I never thought...we never thought we'd need to."

Her friend sat down hard in her chair. "I was hoping it wasn't, but I had a suspicion it might be. The man came in as you saw, trying to sell a shipment. I asked him to bring in a sample so I could be sure. Said he's from Tucson, a new merchandiser. And since we didn't have your inventory—well, I thought I would check. We need to provide something to our customers, and I was hoping this wouldn't be yours."

Olivia tried to catch her breath as she sat in the chair next to Suzanne's desk. "Joe and I went to the ranch and we found nothing. Not as if it had burned, but it was—gone," she said as she hung her head. "I didn't even consider it had been stolen."

Suzanne reached for Olivia's hand. "Olivia, there must be some way we can prove that it was stolen. Something. Your brand, some way to identify your inventory."

"Now that you mention it, everything was gone. Including Percy."

"Percy!" Suzanne exclaimed. "Could he have had anything to do with this?"

Suzanne and Olivia looked up at Mrs. Allen as she spoke from the open doorway.

"Maybe a better way to approach this would to be to question the man who has your inventory. Find out where he got it, and maybe connect that to a theft?" she said as she pulled her gloves off, one finger at a time. "Now that you know it wasn't burnt in the fire, there are things we can do."

"Yes, yes, of course. I told the man to come back tomorrow with the remainder of the purchase, and if we can find out by then, we—"

"We can return it to its rightful owner," Mrs. Allen finished, her eyes twinkling.

"I didn't see any branding irons when I was out there. They were gone, too, now that I think about it." Olivia twisted her hands as Mrs. Allen frowned.

"It would seem that if we had your branding irons—and could find the brand they laid over it, that might do the trick, at least to prove it was stolen. We'd still have to find out by whom, though." Mrs. Allen tapped her chin as she looked out the mercantile window.

Olivia's heart lifted a bit. If she could find a branding iron and show the inventory had been stolen, at least she might have something to sustain her since she had to leave Joe. She ached to tell Suzanne and Mrs. Allen what had happened, but if she only had twenty-four hours to find proof, she needed to get back to the ranch as quickly as possible. And if she didn't leave now, she wouldn't make it before the monsoon arrived—or the sun set.

"Suzanne, I have to go search the ranch again and don't have time to take a buggy. A horse and saddle would be much faster. If I did that, I could be back before dark, not just have arrived at the ranch. And we could get this settled once and for all."

"But, your dress..."

Olivia looked down at her petticoats and skirt. She lifted it up a bit and held her foot out. "At least I wore full length stockings today. I thought it might rain."

Suzanne sighed. "Well, you *are* a married woman, after all," she said slowly as she called for their helper, Liam, to bring around and saddle the fastest horse.

Olivia hung her head. She should tell Suzanne and Mrs. Allen that she would only be a married woman for mere moments longer, but it wasn't the time.

Mrs. Allen's smile sparkled. "While you do that,

I'll track down the man who brought the inventory in and see what he has to say for himself."

"Might that be dangerous? I don't think either one of you should do these things on your own." Suzanne's blue eyes clouded as she looked from Mrs. Allen to Olivia.

Mrs. Allen patted her reticule and winked at Olivia. "I'll be fine, don't worry about me." She turned on her heel and hurried down Allen Street, toward the hotel the man was most likely staying at.

"Suzanne, are you certain? I can send Liam with you. Or run and get Joe..."

Olivia held up her palms to stop Suzanne. She'd already gotten Joe in enough trouble, not just for one day but forever. The last thing she'd willingly do is drag him into *her* trouble when he had plenty of his own to sort out.

"Please, no. I'm just running out to see what I can find that might help. I'm not even sure what I'll find, but there's no danger except the passage of too much time. I must hurry!"

"I wish you wouldn't do this alone, Olivia. It could be dangerous," Suzanne pleaded as Olivia hopped into the saddle, pulling her skirts aside. She knew she shouldn't, but she didn't care what anyone thought. Her future was at stake, and if she could, she'd keep her promise to her father. As she urged the horse to ride faster, she blinked away the tears threatening to spill. Everything in her world had changed, and she had no one to rely on but herself. And she had to somehow make it right.

CHAPTER 34

Olivia turned away as she rode past what just a few short hours before was her home with Joe. The colorful flowers that swayed in the breeze held no joy for her now. She'd never go back. There was nothing left for her there.

She turned her gaze forward toward the ranch, narrowing her eyes and struggling to focus only on the job at hand. She spurred the horse faster, wondering what she had missed when she and Joe had searched the ranch. She hoped there was something that would prove that what she had worked so hard for, she and her father, was hers. It would change everything.

Houses became fewer and farther between as she reached the outskirts of Tombstone. The infrequent shade trees gave way to cactuses, Mesquite, and the yellow-green palo verde trees that dotted the landscape outside of town. The rushing wind loosened her hair, and the quick braid she'd thrown her long, dark locks into flapped on her back. She wanted to throw off her bonnet, but thought she might see better in the sun with it on and the ties flew behind her against her neck as she spurred the horse faster.

The last house she passed gave her pause. As she approached the small neatly kept house with the white picket fence, she sat up in the saddle. Even from a bit of a distance, she saw Joe's grandmother in her rocking chair, her vivid shawl catching the light of the sun as it peeked through the storm clouds. Her heart ached to tell Mrs. Stanton what had happened. Her blood coursed through her veins, and her ears rushed with the words Joe's mother had spoken.

Her heart skipped a beat as Mrs. Stanton stood. Olivia pulled up on the reins of the horse as Mrs. Stanton smiled at her and flagged her down. Surely she should stop for a moment.

Dust billowed around her, and she stifled a cough as she pulled the horse to a stop in front of the white picket fence. Mrs. Stanton pulled her shawl around

THE BLACKSMITH'S MAIL ORDER BRIDE

her and hurried down the steps of the broad porch, lemonade on the table.

"Olivia, darling, where are you off to in such a hurry?" Mrs. Stanton asked as she reached down to open the gate. Olivia hopped down from the horse, running her hand along its mane as she looked down at her dirty boots.

She ran the leather lead through the ring on the post at the side of the gate. She brushed the dark hair that fell into her face aside with the back of her hand as she walked over to Mrs. Stanton. "I'm on my way to the ranch, Mrs. Stanton. It seems that all the inventory Pa and I put together was stolen. Somebody tried to sell it to Suzanne at the mercantile."

Mrs. Stanton gasped, holding the back of her hand to her mouth. Her eyebrows rose as she looked back toward town. "I wish I could say that the scoundrels didn't surprise me anymore after all these years. I've seen some pretty rotten things in my day, but stealing a girl's life's work is...well, rotten." She crossed over to Olivia and drew her into her arms. "Is there anything that I can do to help, my dear?"

Olivia hung her head. She wanted dearly to tell this kind woman what had happened with her mother-in-law. Her heart ached at the words the younger Mrs. Stanton had thrown at her. But there was nothing that anyone could do. There was no reason to share her burden with this kind old woman.

She looked up into Mrs. Stanton's comforting brown eyes. Joe favored his grandmother, the same kindness resonating in his eyes as Olivia now saw in Mrs. Stanton's. She didn't want to hurt either one of them, and it was best just to be on her way.

"It certainly is a dirty deed," Olivia said as she looked out toward the ranch. The storm clouds parted and the sun beat down on the two of them. Olivia lifted her hand to shade her eyes as she looked toward the ranch. Mrs. Stanton's house was one of the last on the outskirts of Tombstone, and when she got back on the horse she'd be out in the open range. She looked to the saddlebags on the horse, and her eyes grew wide as she realized she'd left her gun at the blacksmith shop. She should have asked Suzanne for one, but there was no way she could turn back now. Dust rose on the horizon, and she spotted several horses and riders in the distance. But she had to go ahead, no matter what danger was in store for her.

She turned back to Mrs. Stanton and nodded. "Well, I best be on my way. I need to see if I can find out what happened to Percy, too."

Olivia reached for the lead and pulled the leather through the ring on the post. She stopped as Mrs. Stanton rested her hand on her arm, slowly pulling her around. "Olivia, why isn't Joe with you?" Mrs. Stanton asked softly.

Olivia hesitated, her heart bursting with pain. Her breath hitched as she looked up once again into Mrs. Stanton's kind eyes.

"Mrs. Stanton, Joe...Joe is better off without me. Look at all this mess I've got at the ranch. And the shop...it's his life, and ..." Olivia couldn't bear the concern in Joe's grandmother's eyes and looked down at her dirty boots.

The older woman reached up and brushed a tear from Olivia's cheek. She cupped Olivia's chin and lifted her face up to meet her gaze.

"Something's happened, hasn't it? Is it his mother? Has she interfered?"

Olivia turned away and looked toward the horizon, toward the ranch. "Mrs. Stanton, there's nothing to be done. Joe is better off without me. I'll be on my way."

She gave Mrs. Stanton a weak smile and mounted the horse. She tied her bonnet more tightly under her chin as Mrs. Stanton rested her hand on her knee.

"Olivia, I've never seen Joe this happy. Not since his father died, certainly, and now that you've come along, he's got that old spring in his step again. His smile has returned, my dear, and it's because of you," she said slowly. "He loves you, and I'd venture to guess that you feel the same about him."

Olivia's heart threatened to beat out of her chest. Did Joe actually love her? She'd hoped so, but after what she'd heard today it didn't matter. None of it mattered. If he stayed with her, he'd lose his shop and his family.

"Mrs. Stanton, it's for the best. Joe has his life and I have mine. It was all a big mistake."

"Darling..." Mrs. Stanton started, but Olivia flicked the reins and tapped her heels against the horse, spurring it toward the ranch. And her future.

CHAPTER 35

"Where could she be?" Joe asked of no one as he paced in front of the blacksmith window. He'd rushed back from his mother's house as quickly as he could to tell Olivia the good news. He'd never felt more alive, certainly since his father had died, and he couldn't wait to tell her that they would have a future on their own, without his mother in it.

He wondered if his grandmother knew quite how bad his mother was. Or at least how bad she'd become since his father had passed. The Widow Samson's influence certainly hadn't been a very good thing for their family at all. He wished that he could have one conversation with the mother that he remembered from when he was a boy. That woman could never even consider doing something like this. Not to him, and not to the woman he loved.

But this woman, this woman deserved to be alone. After what she'd done to Will and Carol, and now what she was willing to do to him, she'd made it clear where her loyalties were. And it wasn't with her sons.

He ran his hands through his hair as he looked up and down Allen Street. Olivia had left hours ago to go fetch them lunch. His stomach grumbled as if on cue. Where could she possibly be? He leaned over the edge of the boardwalk, looking up toward the mercantile. He blinked a few times as Suzanne rushed out of the building, down the steps from the boardwalk and across the street. Almost at a run, she stopped when she reached him. He took in a deep breath at the look of concern on her face, and rushed forward. As he tipped back his hat, she caught her breath.

"Joe, it's terrible," she said as she wrung her hands, her knuckles white.

"What is it, Suzanne?" Joe asked as he stepped closer.

"Oh, Joe. It's just as we suspected. The man who

came into the mercantile to offer us the pork products we were to buy from Olivia brought in a sample. The brand is a bit different, but it's clearly from the Double Barrel Ranch. It was stolen, and they're trying to sell it as theirs."

Joe took a step back and swept his hand over his forehead. How could this be? He and Olivia had searched the ranch and found nothing. No remains of anything at all—but maybe that was the problem. They'd assumed it had all burned when in fact it was gone. Stolen.

"Who's responsible for this?" he said, thoughts of his mother and the blacksmith shop immediately swept away. This was Olivia's life, her home, her property, and it was more important to him than anything he had.

Suzanne pulled a handkerchief from the sleeve of her calico day dress. "We don't know. Mrs. Allen has gone to speak with the man who brought in the sample," she said as she pulled her eyes from Joe's and looked up the street.

"And Olivia?" Joe asked slowly. Suzanne wouldn't have come to him unless Olivia was involved. What had she done?

"Oh, Joe, that's why I'm here. Olivia was very,

very upset. She rushed out to the ranch on horseback, hoping to find something to prove that the pork was hers. A branding iron, something. Anything."

He stood and paced. "She went alone?"

"I tried to stop her, Joe. Truly I did. I suggested I come fetch you and you could go with her. She wouldn't allow it. Got on her horse and rode out."

He looked around wildly. He didn't have a key to the shop any longer, but he fingered the key to the livery in his pocket. He'd forgotten about that when he'd had the altercation with his mother.

"Luke, saddle up the fastest horse in the livery," he shouted toward his assistant. "She's headed to the ranch?"

"Yes," Suzanne said. "And there's no telling what's waiting for her out there. At least she has her shotgun."

Joe stopped short, turning toward the corner of the livery where he'd hidden Olivia's gun. He hesitated for a moment, then stalked over and uncovered it, hefting it under his arm. The weight surprised him—heavier than he remembered a shotgun being. He hadn't held one since before his pa died—at his mother's request—but none of that mattered now. What mattered was his wife, and her safety.

"She doesn't, but she will soon," he said as he tipped his hat at Suzanne on his way to the horse that Luke held for him.

CHAPTER 36

Joe shook his head slowly as he headed out of town. He'd never suspected that the inventory had been stolen, and he didn't think she had either. He'd just been enjoying his time getting to know his new wife, who he'd learned was kind, sweet and fascinating. Each day they'd been together, he'd been surprised and delighted to find out something new about her.

Now, as the wind whipped past his ears on his way to her ranch, he realized she was much more. He knew she was bold, courageous and determined —but this could be dangerous.

He sped through the streets of Tombstone, ignoring the shouts and jeers of wagon drivers and cowboys as he weaved through them as fast as he could to reach the outskirts of town.

One of the last houses was his grandmother's, and as he approached, he couldn't miss her bright shawl as she tugged it around her. He'd planned to just wave as he passed, anxious to get to Olivia, but she waved her arms wildly, her tiny figure frantically trying to get his attention.

"Joe, thank goodness you've come. It's Olivia..." She held her hand to her chest as she caught her breath. Joe dismounted, looping the reins through the brass ring. He crossed over to the white gate of the picket fence and took his grandmother's hands in his.

"What is it, Grandma? What about Olivia?"

She fanned herself as she looked up at Joe. "She's on her way to the ranch, to try to find Percy and see about a branding iron. Something about the pork being stolen."

"Yes, I know all about it, Grandma. I'm heading out to help her right now, and I really am in a hurry." His horse stomped its feet anxiously, ready for the road. He squeezed her hands and turned back toward the horse.

She reached for his sleeve and pulled him back toward her. "There's something else, Joe. Something is troubling her, and I'm not quite sure what it is. She said that you'd be better off without her, that she needed to make her own way."

Joe pushed his hat back on his forehead and met his grandmother's eyes. He frowned, wondering what Olivia could have been talking about. Hadn't they been enjoying getting to know each other? What could have happened? Certainly she couldn't know of his mother's ultimatum.

He rubbed the back of his neck as he ran through the days' events in his mind. Olivia had gone home to make lunch for him. She hadn't returned, and he'd gone looking for her—and found his mother and his aunt. Had she run into them, too, before she'd gone to the mercantile?

His stomach sunk at the thought of what they might have said to her. "Did she mention what had upset her, besides the pork?"

"No, she wouldn't say. But it was something about you. I tried to tell her that you loved her, but..."

"Grandma!" Joe exclaimed as his eyes widened.

"What? You do, and you know it. It's as plain as the nose on your face, boy, and you may as well tell her. She's determined to get this pork business sorted out, so hurry and help her so we can get on with things. I'd like some great-grandchildren before it's my time to meet my maker."

He rubbed the stubble on his chin as his cheeks warmed.

"Yes, she's determined—and bold and courageous. That's what I love about her."

"There. I knew it," she said as she looked over to the horse, her eyes widening. "Is that a shotgun in your saddlebag, son?"

His cheeks burned even hotter as he pulled his hat down over his eyes and nodded. "Yes, it's Olivia's. Thought she might need it," he said as his gaze didn't leave hers.

She nodded slowly, her eyes twinkling as she turned and rushed into the house. Moments later, she struggled through the door and down the porch steps, a heavy shotgun in her arms.

"Here, take this," she said as she held out the gun. "It was your pa's."

Joe hesitated. "I'm not sure that's such a good idea, Grandma. Ma—"

His grandmother silenced him with a wave of her hand. "You leave that woman to me. Now, hurry. Go get that girl of yours. She needs you."

Joe leaned forward and pecked his grandmother on her cheek, his heart full.

His Olivia was determined, all right. And he had said that's what he loved about her—loved? He'd said it. And he meant it. She had changed him, shown him courage, conviction and kindness, and it was up to him to tell her. To help her. To sort out their future. And nothing would stop him.

CHAPTER 37

The rain clouds had scattered and the relentless sun beat down on Olivia. She hadn't been riding long, but her horse showed signs of fatigue and she scouted for a water hole. Finding none, she slowed as she approached the San Pedro River. This was the time of year when it pushed against its banks, the product of the frequent rains and flash flooding. She dismounted and led the horse—she couldn't believe she hadn't even stopped to ask his name—to the river's edge.

She sat beside him as he drank, cupping her hands and savoring some of the cool, fresh water. As much of a hurry as she was in, it wouldn't do to have the horse tire before she made it to her destination.

This part of the river was dotted with clumps of

cottonwoods, providing ample shade—there would be plenty of desert to cross later. She rested for a brief moment, working hard at keeping flashing images and bits of conversation from her mind. She'd have ample time to worry about that later—after she had searched the ranch for a branding iron and for Percy.

"You ready, boy?" she said as she reached for the horse's reins. He lifted his head and walked away from her, toward a tree standing beside the river.

"Come on, now. I don't have time for this foolishness." Hands on her hips, she slowly walked behind the horse as he approached the tree and stopped.

He turned and looked at her, his big brown eyes unblinking. Olivia approached and picked up the reins. Her hand stopped in mid-air as she heard a long, low guttural sound. She reached up toward the saddle bag before she remembered it was empty—she didn't have her gun.

The horse whinnied and bobbed its head at the tree. Olivia heard the sound again and she held her breath. This time it sounded more like a groan. If it was a wounded animal, she'd best be on her way.

Horse hooves thudded on the road behind her and she tensed. She'd been hoping she wouldn't find anybody on the road today, that she could get in and out of the ranch in a hurry. She squared her shoulders, hoping that whoever was coming down the road behind her was friendly. Maybe if she was lucky they wouldn't even notice her down by the river, a little bit away from the road.

She wasn't quite sure how she felt when the rider rounded the bend at breakneck speed, his coat flapping in the hot breeze. He was on her horse—Georgie—and his hair touched his collar from under his hat.

Joe.

Her instincts from growing up on the ranch and avoiding danger told her to step back into the shadows and let him pass. She was on a mission, and the conversation they'd likely need to have could wait for another time.

But her heart had other ideas, and she ran forward into the sun, waving at him until he stopped and guided Georgie down the small bank to where she'd stopped.

He hopped off Georgie and took two long strides toward her, taking off his hat. He stopped inches away from her, and she could feel his warm breath on her cheek as his chest heaved.

"Olivia, how could you do this without me? It's dangerous," he warned, his eyes narrowed.

He clearly hadn't heard the news from his mother, that he had to choose between the shop or her, or he wouldn't be here. He'd make the obvious choice for himself and for Will and Carol, and let her go.

She took a step back, away from his warm breath and kind eyes. She'd need to tell him the truth.

"Joe, there's something you don't know. About your mother. About the shop."

She frowned, and irritation swept through her as he laughed.

"Are you going to tell me that my mother is selling the shop unless we have our marriage annulled?"

Her head jerked up and she looked into his twinkling eyes. How could he be laughing at a time like this? Unless he didn't care about her. Unless this was what he wanted. In that case, she'd better get back on the road and find those branding irons.

"Yes, that's what I overheard her talking about when I went home—I mean, to your house—to fetch lunch. I was certain that you'd accept her offer, as you should. It's your life's work, Joe. I am a newcomer. It's not worth the trade."

She turned from him and walked toward the water's edge, stopping at the bank. She heard Joe's grandmother's voice on the wind, telling her that she loved Joe and in this moment, she knew she did. What else would cause this unbearable pain in her heart as she set him free?

She hung her head as he rested his hands on her shoulders and turned her around to face him. Teardrops darkened her dress as they tumbled down her cheeks.

He cupped her chin and lifted it toward him, untying her bonnet and lifting it gently from her dark, braided hair.

She couldn't meet his eyes. Her heart would break if she did, and she wanted him to be happy. Will and Carol, too. And they wouldn't be, because of her.

"Olivia, look at me," he coaxed as he lifted her chin higher.

She took in a deep breath and opened her eyes, her dark eyelashes fluttering for a moment before she saw his sweet smile, laugh lines creasing his eyes.

"There has never been, nor will there ever be, anyone so perfect for me on God's green earth. How I was so fortunate to be there on that fateful day when you needed livery for your horses, I'll never know. But I will be forever grateful."

He leaned forward and placed his warm lips gently on hers as he brushed away her tears.

She opened her eyes again to another smile, and she sighed. "Joe, are you certain? You'll have nothing."

"Olivia, I'll have everything I want. Everything I need. And more," he said as he drew her to him, wrapping his strong arms around her.

She felt him tense, his arms dropping to his sides. "That is, if you'll have me, of course," he said, his face tight and his eyes hopeful.

She placed her hand on his cheek, this man who'd pulled her out of the ashes that her life had become. His deep brown eyes were so earnest, so loving—and they had been since the moment they'd met, now that she thought about it.

He hadn't hesitated one second to marry her, covered head to toe in soot. If there ever was a "for better or worse", that would have been it.

Her chest heaved as she was overcome with love and gratitude. Would she have him? She knew now she couldn't live without him, and she laid her head on his chest for a moment, the beat of his heart matching hers. She lifted her head, reaching up and pulling his face down to her as she placed her lips on his, softly and gently.

She was lost in him, and startled when he broke away, stiffening as he looked toward the horses.

"I think that man might be in trouble," Joe said as he pointed over her shoulder to the tree where her horse stood.

Olivia spun and narrowed her eyes. "Percy!" Olivia cried. She lifted her skirts and ran toward the man on the horse as it came out into the opening and he sagged to the left, dangerously close to falling face down in the dirt. His weak smile faded and his eyes closed just as Olivia reached him.

She reached up and took his arm. Joe rushed up behind her and centered him in his saddle.

"Percy. Percy!" Olivia cried as she frantically grabbed at his shirt. "Is he...is he..."

Joe put his hand to Percy's forehead.

"No, he isn't," Joe said as he looked up at the road. "He's out cold, though. Nasty wound to his knee. Think we can get him to town?"

"We'll have to," Olivia said as she reached in the saddlebags and pulled out a rope she'd hoped would be there. She handed it to Joe and she loosened Percy's collar as Joe tied him to the saddle. "Andy is a good horse and we should be fine, but we'd best hurry."

"Is there another rope? I'd like to tie this a bit tighter."

Olivia crossed to the other side of the horse and as she reached into the saddle bag, her hand closed around something cool—and metal. Her eyes grew wide as she pulled out two metal rods.

"Joe, look," she said as she held them out to him slowly.

"The branding irons," he said, his eyebrows rising as she held out the two long pieces of metal.

"Yes, the Double Barrel Ranch branding iron and another one. The BBB brand of the thieves," she said slowly as she glanced from the branding irons to Joe, and then to Percy.

CHAPTER 38

Olivia led the way back to town, Joe behind her and Percy's horse trotting behind as Joe held his lead. They couldn't travel too fast, but they'd wrapped his wound and they moved as quickly as they could.

Still reeling from the sight of him after all this time, her thoughts raced as they turned up toward Tombstone, away from the river. He was such a good friend of her father's, and she prayed he'd be all right. But now she had so many questions. Where had he been? Where was he the night of the fire? How had the branding irons ended up in his saddle bags?

She shook the thoughts out of her head. They'd just have to wait until Percy came to to ask him anything at all. If they could get him out of the heat and some water in him, maybe that would be sooner rather than later.

Her head prickled as the sun pierced her bonnet and it wasn't a moment too soon that she saw the first houses dotting the landscape outside of Tombstone. Percy still hadn't moved a muscle as they rode, and as they neared Joe's grandmother's house, one of the first on the outskirts, she turned around to see Joe's hat pulled down, his eyes narrowed and focused on the road ahead. Georgie had started to lag, and the horse Percy was on didn't look much stronger.

"How about we stop at Grandma's and get some water for the horses. It'll just take a second and then we can ride on into town," Joe said as he pulled his hat down further to ward off the sun.

Her stomach clenched at the thought of a delay. Percy needed a doctor, and she needed to get those branding irons to Suzanne—or the sheriff. She hadn't decided quite what to do as she didn't know who stole the inventory. At least she could prove that it was hers, and Suzanne had said the man wasn't coming back until the next day. A water stop might be good for all of them, and she waved as they approached, Joe's grandmother in her usual position on the porch.

"Oh, my, what have you got there?" his grandmother asked as she rushed down the porch stairs and through the gate, straight over to Percy.

"Our ranch hand looks like he's seen some better days," Olivia said as she dismounted and threw her reins through the brass ring of the hitching post. "Looks like he's been shot, and he has both of the branding irons I was looking for. We need to get him and the branding irons into town as quickly as possible."

"It certainly is Percy, and he sure *has* seen some better days," Joe's grandmother said as she inspected the unconscious man tied to the saddle. She pulled up the makeshift bandage they'd fashioned and cocked her head. "He's lost a fair bit of blood, but the bullet went straight through. Not much to do for him but clean it and have him rest up," she said as she started to untie the rope.

"Mrs. Stanton, I think we'd better take him to the doctor," Olivia said slowly as she reached for her gun.

Mrs. Stanton's hands fell to her hips. "My dear, I've cleaned more wounds like this than that dimwit doctor has seen in his short lifetime," she said as she cocked an eyebrow. "You two just get him in the house and go on about your business.

Olivia stole a quick glance at Joe and shrugged her shoulders.

"He'll be fine here, Olivia, and we can get to the sheriff quicker," Joe said as he untied the last knot of the rope that held Percy to the saddle.

They wrestled him down from the horse as gently as they could. They each took one of Percy's arms and tugged him through the white picket fence and up the porch stairs, setting him on Mrs. Stanton's divan.

Olivia loosened his collar again and had started to take off his boots when Mrs. Stanton rushed in from the kitchen. "You two shoo, now. I have water on to boil and a bottle of whisky if I need it. For medicinal purposes, of course," she said as she herded them to the door.

Percy groaned before they reached the door, and Olivia turned back. "Percy? Percy, it's Olivia. You're going to be all right."

Percy raised his hand to his forehead and his eyes fluttered. It took a moment for him to focus, but as his eyes rested on Olivia, he smiled. "Did you find the branding irons?"

"Yes, yes, we did. We're taking them into town to

the sheriff. Percy, who did this to you?" Olivia said as she brushed the sweat and grime from his face with her handkerchief.

"I...I don't know. It all happened so quickly. They wore masks and I didn't recognize the voice of the one who shot me. I passed out at first, and when I came to, I couldn't stand up."

"Oh, goodness, I'm so sorry, Percy. Thank you for trying. We think we know where the inventory is, though, and with the branding irons you brought, we can prove that it belongs to us." Olivia stood and paced in Mrs. Stanton's parlor. "Joe, even though we don't know who did this, we have the branding irons. Maybe Mrs. Allen got some information from the man who tried to sell it."

Mrs. Stanton headed into the kitchen, returning with clean cloths and a steaming bowl of water. "You two run along, now. You'll have plenty of time to talk later. See what the sheriff has to say about all this."

Joe grabbed Olivia's hand and pulled her toward the door. "He's in good hands, Olivia. Let's head out," he said as he pulled her down the porch steps.

She looked back over her shoulder at the house. This turn of events certainly wasn't anything she'd expected. She had more questions for Percy, but for now, she knew what she needed to to prove that the inventory was hers. Maybe she'd be in for some good luck for a change.

"Ride with me. The other two horses are in no condition," Joe said as he held out his hand for Olivia. She hopped on the horse in front of him after she'd made sure the branding irons were secure in the saddlebags, and was comforted by his strong arm around her waist as they headed into town. At least they'd be doing whatever they had to do together.

CHAPTER 39

Men, ladies and children of all types and sizes jostled on the boardwalk along Allen Street as Joe and Olivia turned onto it and entered town proper. Joe tightened his hand over Olivia's on the saddle horn as they approached the mercantile, dust pluming from the carriage wheels and horse hooves that passed them.

They'd decided to go see Suzanne first, before the sheriff, and as they approached, his stomach knotted at the sight of Jimmy Joe Walker and one of his ruffians on the bench on the boardwalk, outside the mercantile. He looked up as they arrived, a sneer spreading across his face, and he leaned over and spit into the spittoon next to the bench, his eyes not leaving Olivia. They'd have to get past him, but at least this time Joe was with her.

She seemed determined to ignore him, and after Joe had helped her down, she reached into the saddlebag and retrieved the two branding irons. She looked up and frowned as Joe narrowed his eyes at Walker and pushed his hat up on his forehead. She reached for his hand and squeezed it, pulling him on the opposite side of their horse, away from Walker's, and they headed up the wooden steps.

As they reached the top of the steps, Walker stood, his eyes round as saucers. "What you got there, little lady?" he said to Olivia, his eyes not leaving the metal in her hands. Just the sound of his voice was enough to cause the people on the boardwalk to scurry, and soon it was just Walker, Joe and Olivia.

"Nothing you'd be interested in," she said as she turned away. "The sheriff will be, though."

Walker took a step back and pulled at his collar, his eyes still on the branding irons. "I thought you said there weren't any left," he whispered loudly to the man standing next to him.

The man shook his head and took a step back, his palms held outward toward Olivia. He walked backward a few more paces, and took a quick look at

Walker before he turned and ran down the middle of the road, toward the Birdcage Theater.

Olivia lifted the branding iron in her hand and looked from it to Walker. He shifted his weight from one foot to the other and pulled his hat down on his forehead. "I'll thank you to hand those over, Olivia," he said, a low and slow growl that made the hair on the back of Joe's neck stand up. He grabbed her and pulled her behind him, taking the branding irons from her hand. He wasn't exactly sure why Walker wanted the irons, but it couldn't be good.

Walker took a step forward on the boardwalk as Joe held Olivia behind him. Walker stopped in front of the door to the mercantile, and Joe blanched as it opened wide.

"I have nothing else to say to you, Will," his mother said as she looked back over her shoulder and stepped out of the mercantile—and straight into Jimmy Joe Walker.

Walker laughed, his gold tooth glinting in the sun. "Well, Mrs. Stanton. Fine timing you have," he said as he grabbed her elbow and pulled her in front of him, wrapping his arm around her neck and pulling out his six-shooter.

"Oh, no," Olivia whispered from behind Joe. "Joe,

just give him the branding irons. He's got your mother."

Joe's breath hitched in his throat as Will stepped out from the mercantile and stopped short, his eyes wide as he held his palms up at Walker and his eyes darted to Joe. "What's going on here?"

"Your brother has something that belongs to me, and I aim to get it."

"My mother has nothing to do with this," Will said as he took a step forward.

"Will, stand back," Joe said as he handed the irons to Olivia and reached into the saddlebag for the shotgun—and he hung his head and fought off a curse as he came up empty. Both shotguns were in the saddlebag on the other horse and he hadn't thought to grab them.

"Joe, he can only want the irons because he was the one to steal the inventory. What other reason could he have?" Olivia whispered as she stepped beside Joe.

"Walker, even if you take the branding irons, we can still prove you stole from Olivia."

"I did no such thing, and you can't prove it. Not if there aren't any irons left. It'd be your word against mine. I said, I'll be needing those branding irons from you, Olivia."

Joe's head spun as he wrestled with indecision. Walker had his mother, but he couldn't give the irons back. This was the man who'd ruined his wife's life, burned her farm and stolen all she had. He couldn't let him get away with it.

"Joe," his mother pleaded, and his heart sunk at her voice. Her eyes were wide with terror as she trembled on the boardwalk.

He felt Olivia's hand on his arm and looked toward her. She nudged her chin down the street, and over Walker's shoulder, Mrs. Allen and Mr. Archer stopped. Mr. Archer held his finger to his lips and made a circle with his hand, encouraging Joe to continue talking.

"Okay, Walker, you win. But first, tell me why you did it," Joe said as Olivia's grip tightened on his arm and they watched Mr. Archer walk to the back of Walker's horse, reach up to his saddlebag and retrieve a branding iron.

"I told you. I didn't do it, and you can't prove that I did, soon as I get those irons back."

"Son, there's nothing that taking those irons is going to help you with. You have a matching one here in your saddlebag. It won't be difficult to confirm that you branded over the Double Barrel

Ranch brand and stole the inventory, selling it as your own."

Walker wiped the sweat off his forehead with the back of his hand as Mrs. Stanton squeaked. "That's not mine. That's not even my horse."

Mr. Archer looked from Walker to the JJW branded on the saddle. "You sure about that? Says JJW right here."

Walker's face reddened and he tightened his arm around Mrs. Stanton. "You mind your own business, Archer. And I ain't fooling, Joe, I'll hurt her if you don't hand over those brands."

"Go ahead and give them to him, Joe," Olivia whispered. "Your mother is much more important than any bacon." She squeezed his hand, her green eyes searching his face.

The crack of a gunshot pierced the air and Joe's heart stopped. Olivia gasped and Will ran forward, wrapping his arms around his mother just as she fainted. Walker screeched, falling to the ground as he clutched his knee.

Joe grabbed Olivia as he looked to Mr. Archer, wondering where the shot came from. Mr. Archer looked in shock, his face red, and Joe followed his wide eyes down the boardwalk, where Mrs. Allen, her lips turned up in a sly grin, placed her pistol back in her reticule.

"She's all right," Will shouted over to Joe, and he wrapped his arms around Olivia, relief flooding his body. She clung to him and buried her face in his shoulder as she shuddered. She felt so right in his arms, and he vowed never to let her come in harm's way again.

"It's all right, Olivia. You're safe. We're all safe."

EPILOGUE

"Next thing you know, the boys will be joining the vigilante brigade," Suzanne said as she took the ham out of the oven in Olivia and Joe's kitchen the following week. "I'm sorry Sadie wasn't there to see it—and to see this, your wedding party."

"She needs to rest now that the baby should be here soon. And the ruckus wouldn't have been good for her," Joe's grandmother said before turning to Joe. "I bet that sure was a sight to behold, your mother standing there with Jimmy Joe Walker's arm wrapped around her neck." She chuckled as she shook her head. "I'm surprised she didn't drop dead right there."

"Mrs. Allen sure surprised me, and it was grand

that Mr. Archer spotted the branding iron in Walker's saddlebag after she'd told him the whole story. Couldn't have turned out better," Joe said as he reached for a biscuit and Olivia slapped his hand.

"We're all just lucky it went the way it did," she said as she set butter onto small china plates painted in vivid flowers.

"It might not have if Percy hadn't lived through the fire and found both of the branding irons," Suzanne said. "Thank goodness for him. Who knew he had it in him?"

"I did," Joe's grandmother said as Percy entered the room. Olivia's eyebrows rose at the sight of him —he'd been to the barber and gotten a shave—and she nudged Joe in the side as Mrs. Stanton batted her eyelashes at him.

"You really saved the day," Mrs. Stanton said. "Mrs. Allen did eventually get that man from Tucson to identify Walker after the fact, but it was just another nail in his coffin."

Percy twisted his hat in his hands as his cheeks colored and he looked from Mrs. Stanton to Olivia. "I didn't see who the thieves were and couldn't help much that way. I did see them re-brand the inventory and hide the branding irons, though, before they left me for dead and I passed out," he said as he smiled at Olivia. "I wouldn't have been able to bring them back if Joe and Olivia hadn't found me when they did. I'd been trying to get back to town for days, and I think I might have met my maker under that tree if they hadn't come along."

"Oh, don't be silly. You're a strapping young man, still. You would have made it," Mrs. Stanton said as she held out a plate of cookies to Percy, who took one shyly as his ears turned pink.

"Must be something in the water," Suzanne whispered to Olivia as she headed into the parlor at the sounds of Lily and Lucy arguing over something.

Olivia set the last fork on the table and turned the flowered dish that held her scalloped potatoes a bit to make sure the porcelain flowers on the lid shone just right by the light of the lanterns. She sighed as Joe came up behind her, wrapping his arms around her waist and resting his chin on top of her head.

"You all right?" he asked softly.

She closed her eyes and patted his hands. She turned and crossed over to the window, parting the curtains and craning her neck to see out to the garden. "I think I will be, yes. Do you think she will?" she said as she pointed to his mother, in her customary place pulling weeds from amongst her flowers. Will and Carol sat on the porch, glasses of lemonade in their hands as Mrs. Stanton worked.

He looked over her shoulder as his eyes clouded. "I don't know. I think it was a pretty big shock, the whole thing."

"Being held at gunpoint? I should certainly think so," Olivia said, one eyebrow cocked.

Joe laughed. "Well, that, and finding out that Grandma owned this house, not her, and Grandma giving it to us as a wedding present."

Olivia shook her head. "You certainly could have knocked me over with a feather. And when she agreed to sell the shop to you and Will and we had the money to buy it after getting the inventory back and selling it to Suzanne...I'm still not certain what to make of it all."

"It's all wonderful. We're now partners in the shop. And we have our own home. And looks like Ma might be coming around as you saved the day."

"I didn't really save the day. I didn't even have my gun with me," Olivia said. She straightened the floral plates on the table and stood back to take a look.

"Sure, you did. Mrs. Allen made a crack shot, but she wouldn't have been able to if you hadn't fixed her gun. Ma knows it. We all know it."

Olivia looked up at Joe, her brows furrowed. "I

never thought about it that way, but I suppose you're right. Although she hasn't said a word to me since."

"I think it's a good idea that she leave to visit her other sister for a while. A trip to Canada could be just the thing she needs. At least she's talking to Will again. It may take a while for her to talk to you and Carol, though."

"Hopefully, that horrid Dorothy Samson won't exert any further negative influence on her while she's gone. You'd think she'd be grateful, after what you both and Mrs. Allen did for her," Joe's grandmother said as she brought the rolls into the dining room, placing them beside the potatoes. She crossed to look out the window and sighed. "You know, there was a time when she was happy. She and your father were very much in love, Joe. I am hopeful she'll remember that, and all will be well."

She placed her hand on Olivia's cheek and looked into her eyes. "I think you're a very good addition to this family, Olivia, and I for one am thrilled that you're here."

"Make that two," Joe said as he rested his arm on Olivia's shoulder.

"Well, I suppose, then, that I would make three," she said as she turned toward Joe and lifted her chin. She rested her hand on his cheek, his deep, dark eyes calming her nerves that had been ablaze as she'd readied for the wedding celebration in her own home.

"The shawl looks lovely on you, dear. I'm pleased I could pass it along to someone worthy," Joe's grandmother said as she headed back into the kitchen.

"Can I steal a moment? Everyone will be arriving soon." Joe grabbed Olivia's hand and pulled her out of the dining room and into the parlor.

"Looks as though it's starting already," Olivia said as she parted the lace curtains to see the doctor help Sage down from the buggy. He never had shown up when Sadie and Tripp had called for him. Olivia didn't know him well, but Joe's grandmother had called him a dimwit. You wouldn't know it from the way Sage Archer stared up at him with so much admiration and awe.

Joe's warm hand caressed her arm and she leaned back into him, her head resting on his shoulders. He'd said he loved her at the river, and she'd never forget the way it set her heart aflutter. Now that they were truly man and wife, she felt the same way every single day, every time she laid eyes on him. His strong arms around her felt natural, and she wondered how she'd been able to breathe a single moment before she knew. Knew what true love was.

As he rested his cheek against hers, Olivia looked out the window at the horizon, toward the ranch where so much had happened. It was hard to believe she'd been homeless and penniless not long ago, and now she felt safer than she ever had in her life.

She tugged the shawl around her more tightly—the golds, reds and blues that she'd come to love every time she saw Joe's grandmother—her grandmother. Her new family and her new home, that was even better than the ranch, because Joe was here with her. And always would be.

The next book is Christmas at Archer Ranch. Click here to find out about Sadie's baby and Maria, the Archer's housekeeper's, past.

Christmas at Archer Ranch

Click here for new release information.

Cindy Caldwell New Release Alerts

ALSO BY CINDY CALDWELL

Newport Beach Series

Now that her kids are grown, widow Jen Watson and her two life-long best friends are looking forward to a summer of fun at her family's beach house. When Jen's family wants to sell it to developers, Jen and her friends do whatever they can to stop it. A heart-warming series about the bonds of friends and family.

Newport Harbor House (Book 1)

Newport Beginnings (Book 2)

Newport Sunrise (Book 3)

Newport New Moon (Book 4)

A Newport Christmas (Book 5)

Newport Nuptials (Book 6)

The Pearl Beach Series

Julia Montgomery and her husband have run their Shell

Shop in the Florida Keys for decades. Well, actually, her husband ran it while she raised the kids. Unexpectedly, she has to figure out how to run it herself, or face the consequences.

The Shell Shop

Shell Shop Secrets

Shell Shop Showdown

Vaquita Beach Series

The Vaquita porpoises in the Sea of Cortez are threatened with extinction, and marine biologist Cassie Lewis has devoted her life to trying to stop that from happening. Join her in this beautiful beach community while she does her best to save the species.

As Deep As the Ocean

As Bright As the Stars

By The Light of the Moon

As Blue As The Sky

The Wild West Frontier Brides Series

(in reading order)

The Chef's Mail Order Bride

The Wrangler's Mail Order Bride

The Bartender's Mail Order Bride

The Teacher's Mail Order Bride

Saffron: Bride of Archer Ranch

Carol: Bride of Archer Ranch

The Blacksmith's Mail Order Bride

Christmas at Archer Ranch

Sage: Bride of Archer Ranch

Tarragon: Bride of Archer Ranch

River's End Ranch

Several years ago, four very good writer friends and I wrote a really fun sweet romance series, River's End Ranch, all set on a destination guest ranch in Idaho. We rotated publishing, one of us every two weeks, resulting in 60 books in total! It was an amazingly fun experience to write in the same world as some very dear friends: Pamela Kelley, Kirsten Osbourne, Caroline Lee and Amelia Adams. Below are links to the books that I wrote in the series, and two boxed sets of my books in the series.

These are in Kindle Unlimited.

Honest Horseman

Gallant Golfer

Discovering Dani

Mischievous Maid

Christmas Catch-Up 5

Cindy Nichols Box Set 1-4

Snickerdoodle Secrets

Bashful Banker

Mistletoe Mistake

Picture Perfect

Cindy Nichols Box Set 5-8

Teaching Tamlyn

Fanning Flames

Christmas Catch-Up 10

Cindy Caldwell books in the American Mail Order Bride series - 45 authors, 50 states, 50 brides

Josephine, Bride of Louisiana

Michelle, Bride of Mississippi

Printed in Great Britain
by Amazon